LJB
W9-BGW-452

Praise for *The Collector*

"The plot is unexpected, original and takes you by surprise."

—*Elle Magazine (Readers Panel)*

"The story is captivating, with twists and turns and murders, along with a dive into the little-known world of art specialists and counterfeiters."

— *Elle Magazine (Readers Panel)*

"A well-written plot with all the necessary ingredients: a few deaths, lost objects and a whole collection of worrisome characters…Ideal for a moment of relaxation."

— *Elle Magazine (Readers Panel)*

"A good first mystery set in the cut-throat world of art collectors. Anne-Laure Thiéblemont depicts well the power struggles, scams and greed, and pulls readers in with the story of poor Marion Spicer who didn't ask for anything."

—*L'Ours Polar*

"A writer to follow. A well-researched and very effective mystery."

—*La Provence*

"Anne-Laure Thiéblemont has written a fine first mystery set in the shifty world of art collecting. She respects some of the genre codes, but also breaks from them with an unexpected tone and rich characters. A good fix."

—*Lire*

"As much a mystery as an identity quest, with tight suspense and strong writing, this debut novel by an experienced art reporter reveals her qualities as a writer with a promising future."

—*Playboy*

"I am a big mystery fan, and this book fills the bill. Unlike a lot of "American cozy mysteries", this one is intelligent and cerebral as well as a true thriller. It also leaves you wondering, based solely on names, if we aren't part of the ruse. That's what brings me back to this publisher."

—Goodreads

"I loved this fast paced exciting thriller. Marion is an intelligent and likeable heroine and I hope to see more of her in the future."

—Librarian review

The Collector

Anne-Laure Thiéblemont

Translated from French by Sophie Weiner

LE FRENCH BOOK

All rights reserved: no part of this publication may be reproduced or transmitted by any means, electronic, mechanical, photocopying or otherwise, without the prior permission of the publisher.

First published in France as
Le Collectionneur
by Editions Liana Levi
©2006 Editions Liana Levi

English translation ©2015 Sophie Weiner
First published in English in 2015
by Le French Book, Inc., New York

http://www.lefrenchbook.com

Translator: Sophie Weiner
Translation editor: Amy Richards
Proofreader: Chris Gage
Cover designer: Jeroen ten Berge

ISBNs:
Trade paperback: 9781939474445
Hardback: 9781939474469
E-book: 9781939474452

This is a work of fiction. Any resemblance to actual persons, living or dead, is purely coincidental. For the purposes of the story, the author took authorial license with references to historical events, places, facts, and people.

F THI
1797 3044 9/22/15 LJB
Thiâeblemont, Anne-Laure,

The collector
ABJ

To Michel

One evening, I sat Beauty in my lap.
And found her bitter. And I cursed her.
—Arthur Rimbaud

LeRoy Collins Leon County
Public Library System
200 West Park Avenue
Tallahassee, FL 32301

PROLOGUE

In the sparsely furnished room, the air thick with smells of alcohol, sweat, and stale cooking fat, the girl whimpered as he pinned her down with his leg and blindly groped for something beside the bed. He fumbled until he found it: a terra-cotta figure.

The man smiled faintly while he caressed the cold almond eyes and prominent nose with fingers that were long and thin, like an artist's. He tensed when he couldn't find the metal ring in the sculpture's nostrils, then relaxed when he made contact. He brushed his hands over the cold emeralds and along the notches on the right side of the figure, like ritual markings that bridged the gap between him and his sculpture, his *Tattooed Man*, which stood erect on the dirt floor.

Still fondling the object, he turned his attention to the girl, who was crying now. He pulled himself upright and clutched at her. The iron bed screeched and banged against the wall as he tried to heave himself onto her. She kicked and swatted at him. Just as she struck his face, which already had three long, perfectly symmetrical scars, he released his hold and collapsed on top of her, convulsing, and mumbling incoherently.

~ ~ ~

She waited, suspended in silence under the mass of flesh. A few seconds went by before she realized what had happened and pushed the dead weight off her. She rushed out of the house and into the night.

When the body was discovered half an hour later, the sculpture was gone.

1

"The collection is this way."

His tone was dry and not particularly welcoming. Standing before her in the parlor, he gave her the chills. His gray reptilian eyes showed no emotion, and his long face seemed cut from ivory. His right hand was sunk deep in the pocket of his night-blue blazer and refused to budge—not even to greet her.

George Gaudin had been Edmond Magni's personal assistant until a week ago, when, somewhere in Peru, Magni had mysteriously dropped dead—for the second time in Marion's life.

The first time, her mother was the one to announce the news. "He died in a plane crash," she had told Marion. It was a lie. In truth, her husband had abandoned his family and his given name, Jean Spicer, and had assumed a new identity.

From the age of three, Marion had gotten by without him, believing all those years that her father was dead, without so much as a photo to cling to. Not a single picture of him could be found in their home. And every time she asked her mother to share a story, an anecdote, a memory, the woman would retreat into a silence or fly into a fit that could only be remedied if she isolated herself in her bedroom and slept.

Marion stopped asking questions.

Now, thirty-three years later, out of the blue, an executor had informed her that her father hadn't been dead all those years. He had just made a new life for himself, and she would be inheriting—among other things—one of the greatest collections of pre-Columbian art in the world, valued at over forty million euros. Of course, the inheritance had certain stipulations. Nothing came that easy for Marion.

Gaudin crept to the other end of the room and gestured for her to follow. She had hoped to linger in the immense space. Perhaps it would rouse the memory of a scent, an image, a feeling of déjà-vu—anything to fill the void. But she couldn't find the slightest personal connection.

She hadn't seen so many in one place since watching *Barry Lyndon* in a Stanley Kubrick retrospective. She surveyed the Louis XV-style furniture with its Rococo curves, the brocade fabrics, the brass, the redwood marquetry, the Boulle-work drawers, the Venetian mirrors, and the chandeliers dripping pendants of rock crystal.

A world so unlike her humble childhood.

"This way."

The assistant's directive dripped with arrogance.

Without any further formalities, he disappeared behind a copper-colored silk wall hanging. She followed and discovered a reinforced door that opened to a narrow staircase. She hurried down the steps just as the door closed behind her. It made surprisingly little noise, considering its weight.

Marion stopped at the bottom of the stairs. The space was cold and devoid of light, sound, colors, and smells. She peered into the darkness. It seemed like an unknown abyss, and she had the disturbing sensation that she was being watched.

Gaudin flicked on the lights. A shiver traveled up Marion's spine, and she gasped. In the faint illumination provided by the bulbs, literally hundreds of clay sculptures and vessels took shape. Floor-to-ceiling shelves were lined with odd-looking creatures. Some had hollow eyes, stunted bodies, and swollen arms and legs. Many looked sickly and tormented. They stared at her with lifeless eyes.

Marion's mouth went dry, and her legs began to shake. Eventually she inched closer and examined the sculptures one by one. She knew that some of the pieces were pre-Incan portrait vases. She had never cared for these indigenous works. And in such large numbers, she found them disturbing. Certainly there was nothing aesthetically pleasing about the frozen assembly of cripples in this place.

A second room was equally disquieting, filled as it was with oversized phalluses and female genitalia in every possible position and depiction—pimple-covered erections, clitoris-shaped noses, pumas copulating with toads, skeletal women being sodomized. By the looks of it, Magni had relished the world of sexual obsession. Marion just stared at the impassive expressions on the faces of the silent participants.

"Thousands of years, and these bodies are still here for us to see and touch. Isn't that fascinating?" Gaudin said from behind her.

Marion didn't respond. She could barely breathe. This space was a shrine to her father's obscenity, negotiated at the cost of gutted tombs and stolen memories. And for what? A dark and irrational desire to claim ownership over the souls of the dead? An attempt to give them a second life? Or to extend his own? Was he afraid of something? Or of someone?

Gaudin appeared to take her silence as an invitation to continue. He picked up a female figure and weighed it in his hands.

"Here we have the likeness of a poor woman condemned for her sexual transgressions. Her mind and body are withered away," he said in a clearly feigned tone of compassion. "Debauchery, depravity—this is how she's immortalized."

"That's your opinion," Marion replied harshly. "We don't know enough about these early civilizations to make such judgments. And we certainly don't know anything about her."

"Does it matter? These objects are loved for the imagery they arouse, not necessarily for their *raison d'être*, which no longer exists in any case."

"Whose fault is that? If they hadn't been stolen and hidden away from the world like this, maybe we'd know a bit more about the people who created them."

"A woman of morals," Gaudin snickered. "I can't believe Magni entrusted his collection with someone so naïve."

He started to walk away before she could respond. "Let's go. The tour isn't over yet. I wager you'll be convinced by the end of it."

Her jaw clenched, Marion followed him into the last room.

"Here we are. The Holy of Holies," the assistant said with feverish eyes. "Here we have the most beautiful pieces in the world."

Marion's tension dissolved as she gazed at the room while her tour guide swooped from one breathtaking piece to the next. The floor was covered with intricate lapis lazuli inlays. Soft lights in the showcases illuminated gold metalwork here and a shimmering serpentine mask there. The collection, nearly thirty pieces altogether, was shockingly beautiful. This was nothing like the wild assortment in the first two rooms. Perhaps Magni had become more selective over the years.

"But why? Why such a radical change?" she asked.

"Because all connoisseurs' tastes evolve when they no longer give into the same impulses."

"He could have sold his less valuable pieces. Why did he keep them?"

"They made him who he was. They were his questions, his answers, his qualms. They were his memories. They kept him on track. Having them around reminded him of why he was different."

"Different?"

"He wasn't like other collectors. Most are in it for the prestige, or they're trying to forget where they came from—some are people with no families of note who want to create a new kind of lineage through their acquisitions."

"And what was he after?" she asked as she approached a mask with both shaman and jaguar-like features.

"You have to get closer, much closer. Probe the object, smell it, imagine what lies beneath," Gaudin whispered in her ear.

She swiftly slid away from him.

"Look at it. Such expression, such power in the design. This jade—a mineral harder than steel—was sculpted with ancient tools. Can you imagine?"

"You haven't answered my question. What was Magni's goal?"

"His goal? Ah yes, his goal," Gaudin repeated indifferently. "I could tell you that he wanted to know everything, that he wanted to examine continuities and variations in style. Hmm, what else?

That he had a need to replace something that he lost, maybe something that wasn't there in the first place. Mademoiselle, collecting is a form of lust. There's a burning desire. It's not something you can explain in so many words."

So Magni was no different from other collectors. Marion sighed and turned her attention to Gaudin. He was patronizing her. She couldn't quite figure him out. Although ghostlike and guarded upstairs, he was an entirely different animal underground. The basement aroused him. Now he was animated, and his body language was exaggerated. He was scary, like the figures in the first room. It was as if the sculptures and their protector were fused together. It made her think of Indonesian headhunters harnessing their enemy's life force through preserved heads.

"Let's go back upstairs," she suggested abruptly. "I have to show you some photographs. They're in the living room."

"What photographs?"

"The three sculptures I need to find."

"Three?" he said with a hint of worry in his voice, as if the number were more important than the sculptures themselves.

"You are well aware of the provisions of the will, aren't you?"

"The estate attorney mentioned something, yes, but he didn't specify a number."

"Three, eight, ten. What's the difference? Either way, I'm in a bind. No sculptures, no inheritance."

~ ~ ~

Gaudin sat down on a caramel-colored velvet couch. Behind him was a pink marble fireplace with a fluted surround. There wasn't the trace of an ember in the hearth.

"He hated the sound of wood crackling in a fireplace," Gaudin said.

"He must have been the only person in the world."

"I never liked it either."

Ignoring his reply, she picked up her bag, which had been lying on the floor next to a large parquet table, handed him the three photos, and sat down in a chair across from him. It was as plush as the cushion lining a jewelry box. She exhaled at last. Gaudin could act cross if he wanted; it was more comfortable up here. But the instant she looked over at him she was struck by his alarmed state. His forehead was covered with sweat as he stared at the photos in his lap.

"What is it?" she asked, shifting in her seat.

Gaudin slowly straightened up, and she caught a not-so-reassuring glimmer in his eyes.

"What?" she insisted.

"I didn't know he was looking for them," he finally said.

Marion got up from her chair and moved to a closer one.

"Do you recognize them?"

He nodded.

"They're exceptional pieces from northern Peru." Gaudin cleared his throat before adding, "Very rare, from the Piura region. And they still have their emerald ornamentation. Tomb raiders usually sell the gems separately."

"So you've seen them before? Do you know where they are?"

"They were put up for auction three years ago. It was in June."

"Why didn't Magni acquire them then?"

"He's the one who sold them."

"I don't understand." Marion stood up and started pacing in front of the couch. "I was told that I needed to lay my hands on three sculptures. The attorney didn't say that Magni once owned them. I thought you said he saved everything, that he never let go of a single sculpture."

"That's true."

"Except for these three. He could have sold others without you knowing."

"Those were the only ones."

"So why'd he sell them?"

Gaudin didn't respond. Avoiding eye contact, he crossed and uncrossed his legs.

"Which auctioneer handled the sale?" Marion finally asked, her voice rising.

"I don't remember."

"Of course you don't."

Marion sat down again and thought for a few moments.

"Do you happen to know who bought them?"

"The buyers remained anonymous. They can do that at auctions."

"Do you think I'm new to this? Of course they can, but when you want something, you find it," she said, staring at the personal assistant until he looked at her.

"You have no idea who bought them?" she asked.

"No."

"When did Magni initially purchase them?"

"In January of the same year."

"What? He didn't keep them very long—barely six months. That's strange, isn't it, for someone so attached to his artifacts?"

Obviously, Magni wasn't exactly the man Gaudin was making him out to be.

"And who sold them to *him*?" she asked.

"I don't know."

"Good God, you were his personal assistant."

"Do you think that made me privy to all his secrets?" he answered in a voice so sharp, Marion was forced to release her glare and look away.

I'll never get anywhere with this dude, she thought. And I still don't know anything about my father. Where did his money come from? Did he work? Did he have any friends? The estate attorney had mentioned a stormy relationship with a woman that had lasted ten years. That's all he could say. And this assistant wasn't going to be of any help—he was more of a clam, and maybe even a scared clam.

Gaudin was withholding information. She was sure of it. This was going to be a tough match. He had good reason to keep his mouth shut. As long as those three sculptures remained at large, he would be master of the house and owner of everything in it. That was the second provision of the will. Evidently, this collection was also his. After thirty years of serving Magni, Gaudin would not back down so easily. And yet Edmond Magni didn't designate him as the legatee so the collection could live on. How strange.

2

Marion stepped out of the mansion onto a quiet side street in the sixteenth arrondissement of Paris, one of the city's most exclusive residential neighborhoods, foreign to her, despite the concentration of museums in the area. Her life was so much more ordinary than this, she thought as she headed to metro station. Like the dull clouds crowding the morning sky. Yet Paris had a way of making even gray beautiful.

Needing to clear her head, Marion changed directions, and instead of turning right toward the Passy station, she veered left and headed to the Place du Trocadéro. There, she crossed the gardens, taking in the *Dame de Fer*—France's Iron Lady, the Eiffel Tower—before turning left and following the Seine River to the Parisian Golden Triangle: Avenue Montaigne, with Dior, Chanel, Nina Ricci, wealthy clients, and prestigious auctions.

Finally, Marion Spicer marched into SearchArt. She had barely taken two steps into her office when her boss flagged her down. As usual, she wasn't in a good mood.

"I've been waiting for you. I want you in my office," Françoise Vigan demanded, then slammed the door behind her.

After her mind-boggling visit with Gaudin, Marion was unfazed by her employer's order, a first.

Her natural inclination was to jump at the head honcho's command.

Françoise Vigan was a woman who only grudgingly greeted her employees with a "hello" in the morning. She made her money on the victims of theft—collectors, patrons, bankers, government officials, and lawyers. Investigating stolen art was the firm's specialty.

SearchArt also did business with Christie's, Sotheby's, and a few French auctioneers that didn't have the time or money to thoroughly research the origins of objects they intended to present for bidding. The firm inspected artwork with a fine-tooth comb before reviewing the channels the items had gone through: the antiques dealers, bric-a-brac traders, and appraisers who frequently supplied auctions with stolen goods. SearchArt employees did hands-on investigation and used a vast, inter-agency photo library of stolen objects—two hundred thousand paintings, knickknacks, and pieces of furniture. The database aggregated information on stolen goods from insurance companies, Interpol, the FBI, and the French Banditry Repression Brigade, which had an elite white-collar crime unit dedicated to art theft.

Those who preferred not to declare the theft of an artwork—for whatever reason—were treated in a much more confidential manner. Françoise Vigan profited greatly from well-known names in the art world who didn't want their vulnerabilities exposed. In fact, she was often their last hope. Marion specialized in eighteenth-century furniture, jewelry, silverware, and other objects. In five years, she had succeeded in having twenty-some pieces withdrawn from public auction. Compared with the seven thousand pieces of art stolen in France every year, this was nothing. But in the world of art, her record was impressive.

Most of her cases involved expensive but not-so-rare antiques: roll-top desks, majolica pottery, candlesticks, clocks, eighteenth-century ewers, and Cartier brooches and rings. Verifying their authenticity wasn't always easy. Stolen objects were often doctored before being sold off. The designer markings might be removed or falsified. Clock mechanisms were sometimes altered. Cabinet locks were often changed. Candelabras were refurbished. An antique could quickly become unidentifiable.

Marion could already hear Françoise Vigan's heels clicking just above her head. Her boss, whose office was one floor up, was losing patience. Françoise always stomped whenever she wanted to speak with someone. SearchArt was her personal banana republic.

She'll just have to wait, Marion huffed while scanning in her father's photos to see if the sculptures were in the system. She entered the characteristics in the search engine: "warrior, woman with child, jaguar, pre-Columbian, terra-cotta, emerald," and the recognition feature worked its magic. Twelve pieces appeared on the screen. None of them could be confused with hers. At least hers were not stolen.

Deep in thought, Marion stared at the computer. She had presumed that she had gotten her interest in art—she wouldn't exactly call it a passion—from her mother, who spent much of her time in museums. Her mother had always had a greater connection with the creative world than the real one. She would visit a museum whenever she was feeling blue, and she'd drag Marion along. Eventually, Marion didn't need to be dragged. Now she knew that art also connected her to her father.

As she reviewed Magni's images on the computer screen, it dawned on her that the photos were of an exceptional quality. Zooming in, she was even able to make out the flaws in the stones. The work of a pro, she thought as she turned over the photos one by one. A small label was on the back of each: "Studio 6." Collectors didn't usually have documents that were this good. Theirs tended to be blurry or overexposed, too dark or too bright to make out the details. And often that didn't matter to them. Most collectors thought their objects were unique. In reality, though, one decorated clock looked like many others. One commode could be mistaken for another.

Françoise was still stomping. Marion headed to the stairs.

~ ~ ~

As Marion took a seat in front of her boss's desk, Françoise pretended not to notice and continued signing papers. A few minutes went by before she finally looked up.

Marion sighed. This woman became more ridiculous with each passing day. Françoise had flaxen hair and was tall and scrawny, like a Giacometti sculpture. Over her wiry build she piled layers of loose black tops, which she paired with pencil skirts, also black. And her neck! It was always covered with a thick coiled necklace of pearls or jade, depending on her mood. Masking the many folds and wrinkles, her fine jewelry was like a Medici collar, hence the name her staff had given her behind her back.

"Marion, where are we with the Jeanson file?" La Medici fired.

"We have a problem."

"What is it?" she groaned while giving Marion's ensemble—jeans, sneakers, and a V-neck sweater—a disapproving look. With those clothes, plus her boyish haircut, Marion stuck out in La Medici's staunchly formal setting. The woman surrounded herself with Jean-Michel Franck influences: white walls, Parsons tables, and cube chairs that hurt Marion's back. The room was as stiff as the woman working in it.

"Sotheby's has agreed to withdraw Jeanson's teapot from their sale," Marion explained. "It is easily identifiable with the 'Mons' inscription, the 1743 date, and the animal-shaped spout. Clearly it's his. But the seller's clean. He didn't steal it or buy it from someone who did. He purchased the teapot from an antiques dealer in Amsterdam. There's no way we can implicate him."

"Does he have a receipt?"

"Yes. He's bulletproof. Even though he knows now that the teapot was stolen, he has made it clear that he will not return it. And the law's on his side. Legally, possession is as good as the title. He's the legitimate owner. If Jeanson wants to retrieve his property, he'll have to buy it back."

"How ironic. The law's supposed to protect the victim. In this case it hurts him. So what has Jeanson decided to do? Is he willing to pay?"

"Forty-five thousand euros for an object that belongs to him? He's having a hard time accepting that."

"He can always go after the merchant."

"I don't think he wants to. I think he'd rather believe the object is still his but just living at another man's house."

"All right." Françoise was quiet for a few seconds. "Let it go."

Marion looked at her, stunned. Not even two weeks earlier, the Jeanson case was a top priority. For the first time ever, Françoise had asked Marion to meet with the client and handle negotiations with his lawyer. Françoise never asked staff members to represent the firm. She wanted outsiders to think of SearchArt as hers alone.

With a smile, she handed Marion a red folder.

"I know this is a bit out of your realm, but..."

Marion opened the file and closed it immediately.

"This is way out of my realm," she said. "Bruno handles these pieces."

"This is too delicate a case for him. Don't argue. Just study the file."

"I'm behind on my other work. You'll have to assign this to someone else," Marion responded without losing her cool.

"You're not following me. I want *you* to take care of it and no one else. It's time to familiarize yourself with pre-Columbian art. Since last winter's theft, we're getting more cases like this one. I advise getting over your qualms, if you want to stay with this firm."

~ ~ ~

Back in her office, Marion threw the red file on her desk. What a bitch! Staff members specialized in certain eras and regions for a reason. What was the woman planning to do? Did she intend to hire another eighteenth-century expert? Maybe she was about to fire Bruno.

Marion had no particular attachment to SearchArt. She had wanted to leave for some time but hadn't gotten up the nerve. Marion wasn't a rash or reckless person. She liked order and the slightest change could throw her off. Maybe once she had her inheritance and was rich, she'd be more daring. Only she wasn't rich yet. Yes, an account with two million euros had been opened in her name, but it could only be used to buy the three pieces of art. If the bank noticed even a modest withdrawal for a designer purse—not that she wanted one—her whole inheritance would be taken away.

"First the inheritance, now this case… What a strange coincidence," she muttered before dismissing the idea altogether. La Medici couldn't possibly know. The estate attorney had assured her everything would be kept confidential.

She looked at the stacks of files on her shelves, the floor, and her desk. They were everywhere. That was one good reason she always met clients elsewhere.

Still obsessing over her meeting with La Medici, Marion stepped over and around the papers to reach her desk.

Bruno, who specialized in primitive art and archeological objects, was no novice. He could have easily taken care of this case. Why had it been given to her when she was already drowning in assignments? The eighteenth-century pieces she worked on were the firm's most lucrative. And she excelled in her work. She couldn't remember faces, books, or movie titles, but she could describe in detail the interior of a château ten years after seeing it in a magazine—a clear advantage when so-called owners couldn't even draw up an inventory of the objects they were protecting.

The phone jolted her from her musings.

"Yes, Sophie. Who called? Mr. Rambert. What? He's called three times already? Give me his number. Anyone else? Okay. Do me a favor. Take down all my messages, and say I'm in a meeting. I can't have any more distractions. No, don't worry. Everything's fine."

She hung up. Then, as she collected the papers that had spilled out of the file when she threw it on her desk, a photo caught her eye.

Same size, same sharp focus, same lighting. She turned the picture over: "Studio 6."

The stone shaman's face drew her in. There was something familiar about it. Had she seen it at her father's mansion? She stared at the image, trying to remember the details of the figure in Magni's collection. No luck. Marion cursed her memory's unfortunate habit of disregarding things she wasn't interested in. She leafed through the pages of the file, noting there was no certificate of authenticity.

She did, however, find the client: Laurent Duverger, a certified appraiser for the Paris Court of Appeals. She was aware of the man's reputation. Bruno had told her about him. In the world of pre-Columbian art, Duverger was the go-to guy for expert appraisals. He practically had a monopoly on it.

This file was too sparse. Marion headed over to Bruno's office, which was just across from hers, and opened the door without knocking. Sitting behind his computer, Bruno yelped.

"Shit, Marion. Warn me next time. I thought you were La Medici."

"Are you hiding something?" she teased.

"What do you want?" he mock-pouted in return. "You were late this morning, leaving me all alone with my coffee and the crazy lady upstairs."

"I'm sure you've recovered from the trauma. Hey, I like your tie today. Wide red-and-blue stripes instead of the narrow ones."

"You know me, Marion, always the professional. Don't you think I look stylishly conservative in my gray suit and Oxford tie?"

"Yes, you're a handsome one, Bruno. No doubt about it. I've got a question for you. Have you ever dealt with Laurent Duverger?"

"Sure. Whenever I've got an ID problem, he's the guy I call. He can spot the smallest crack or sign of restoration on any terra-cotta. It's like he's had his hands on every one of them at some point or another."

"That's not what I mean. Have any of his pieces ever been stolen?"

"Maybe. But he's never come to us for help."

"Does he have any special ties with La Medici?"

"Why don't you sit down? You're making me dizzy with all your pacing. And that thing you do with your hands—you know, like you're writing on your palm—that doesn't help."

"Okay, enough with your analyzing all my annoying little habits—I know you really think they're charming. I need your help."

"With what?"

"La Medici just made me take a case from Duverger. It's pre-Columbian. I have a vague idea why she wants me on it."

Bruno gave her a questioning look.

"Don't worry. It has nothing to do with you."

"I'm not worried, just curious. That's usually my department, but there's never any telling with La Medici. Anyway, are you okay? You seem a little tense."

"I'm tired, that's all."

Bruno studied her for a while. "I don't know if they have a special relationship. I've never seen them together. All I know is that Duverger refers his clients to SearchArt when their pieces have been stolen. Sometimes he serves as a go-between."

"So he generates business for us."

"You could say that."

Marion stared out the window for a few seconds and then looked at her colleague. "Do you keep all the auction catalogs?"

"Yeah, I try to." Bruno pointed to the shelves on a wall.

"Can I check them out?"

"What are you looking for?"

"A pre-Columbian art auction from three years ago, in June."

Bruno stood up and walked over to a row of catalogs, which he skimmed with his fingers.

"Are you sure of the year? I've got nothing from then. Maybe it was a no-catalog auction. Do you know who organized it?"

"No. And I'd be surprised if there wasn't a catalog. Edmond Magni sold a few pieces at that auction."

Bruno threw her a sharp look. "Magni? What does he have to do with this?"

"I can't tell you. Not right now."

"You're being very mysterious."

Bruno's predictable display of interest amused her. She could usually confide in him, even though he was always bragging that he knew everything about everyone. But the estate attorney had warned her. For now, it would be best to keep quiet. Giving away her identity could attract all sorts of treasure seekers, and that could mess with her investigation.

Bruno broke the silence. "It could definitely be this one auction, but I don't have the catalog. It was super confidential. Invitation only. I think Mr. Tanglas put it on. I can check if you want."

"Could you send me a copy of the catalog if you find it?"

If it was that auction, and her sculptures were sold there, she'd need the lot numbers. Even with this information, she'd have a hard time getting the buyer's name. She'd have to be sneaky.

"Mind if I pick your brain a few more minutes? I need to know more about Magni."

"What would you like to know?"

"More than just what's been written about him."

"I've only picked up rumors here and there. It's all speculation."

"Tell me anyway."

"They say the truth about a man can be determined by what he's hiding," Bruno began once he had settled into his chair again. "Magni was a master when it came to keeping his professional secrets hidden. He had a great fortune, and no one knows where it came from. He was invisible outside the auction houses and a few art galleries. He avoided private viewings, galas, tennis tournaments, and golf competitions where informal transactions are made. Still, he assembled pre-Columbian art collections for the Louvre, the president, and big manufacturers—and that's just the tip of the iceberg. We know this for sure: he was a guru of his genre, and he created and conquered the market."

"What do you mean?"

"Consider this. Why do we rarely see Chorrera, Veracruz, or Huari pieces in collections? Magni showed very little interest in them. When he bought certain pieces or seemed fascinated with a group or culture, buyers and collectors followed his lead."

"There must have been people who disagreed with him. No one ever questioned him?"

"Up until three or four years ago, no. Now things are different. Duverger's the only one who could have stood up to Magni. He's in cahoots with all these archeologists, and he hangs out with journalists who write about him. To boot, Duverger has great intuition. He can tell a major piece at first sight."

"I'd really like to believe that novice collectors relied on Magni's opinion, but museum curators, with all their expertise, would be able to form their own judgments," Marion said.

"I wouldn't be so sure of that. They tend to follow what other curators do in case any of their superiors question their acquisitions. And curators are all buddy buddy with buyers and collectors who do appraisals for museums. Then the curators organize big shows with pieces that belong to these same buyers and collectors. If the pieces are sold at auction later, they have the pedigree of a prestigious exhibit. See how entangled their worlds are? Their ties are shady, and their networks are so interlinked that if one of them messes up, they're all screwed. It's something they avoid at all costs."

"Okay, so Magni didn't play the game, right?"

"Yeah, and you know the craziest part? He was able to become one of the art world's most recognized and respected collectors without a single soul ever laying eyes on his collection."

"I read that in the paper. I couldn't believe it."

"Ask the appraisers, researchers, and art critics. Some were able to schedule appointments with him, but he never showed up. No explanations provided.

Others got even ruder treatment. Duverger was telling me—"

"They knew each other?"

"Duverger and Magni? Yeah, of course. Duverger sold him a bunch of pieces." Bruno paused. "Listen to this: Duverger told me that one time Magni refused to meet a curator just because the letter requesting the visit arrived with postage due. Magni looked down on everyone. He loved to humiliate people, and he was ruthless. But as much as he kept his professional side hidden, he had quite a reputation. His love of exhibitionism and carnival sideshows was legendary. His little soirées made a lot of noise."

"There must have been something more substantial written about his collection somewhere."

"Magni did just one interview. It was for an American magazine. He insisted that the reporter give him prior approval, and he wouldn't allow any photos. Because no other reporter had been given this kind of opportunity, he agreed to let Magni read the article before it went into print. When the article did appear, it had been thoroughly revised—by Magni, of course."

"Then everything they say about him is true."

"Or false. It's impossible to get an accurate depiction of the guy. Everyone's view of him is skewed. People either admired him or hated him. But nobody really knew him. What's left of him—his collection—that's his only truth. I can't wait to see it!"

Marion diverted her eyes. She couldn't look Bruno in the face for fear she'd give herself away. She forced a smile.

"Thanks for your help."

She got up and started for the door, then turned around.

"I almost forgot! Have you received photos from Studio 6 for any of your cases?"

"Yeah. They're the only good ones I ever get. They all come from Duverger's clients."

~ ~ ~

Marion's brain was in overdrive as she walked across the hall to her office. Her father's sculptures could have been purchased by this appraiser. Maybe her inheritance and the file she had just been given were, indeed, connected. She had barely opened the door when the phone started ringing. It was the internal line.

"Yes, Sophie. I told you. I'll call him back later. Okay, okay, put him through."

She heard a click and then a raspy voice.

"Marion Spicer? This is Mr. Rambert. I'm an auctioneer. I tried calling several times."

"Yes, I got your messages. How may I help you?"

"I heard about your father. My sincerest condolences."

Marion felt her face flush. She tightened her grip on the receiver. The auctioneer continued.

"Edmond Magni was one of our most loyal clients. So if you need an appraiser or an advisor, we're here for you."

Her head was pounding. Her throat was bone dry. She couldn't speak.

"Miss Spicer, are you still there?"

"Yes..."

"It would be my pleasure to—"

She slammed down the phone and pounded the desk with her fist.

"Bunch of vultures," she seethed at the phone. "Jesus, who told them? I should have known."

Marion was too familiar with this world. There was no way she could have kept her inheritance a secret. Of course a collection this important would excite all the treasure-seekers. Unaware of the stipulations in the will, they would be expecting hundreds of sculptures to come onto a market weakened by tighter export restrictions. And Duverger would be the first in line.

She sighed and glanced at the red file again. The appraiser had probably used La Medici. The stolen shaman was an excuse to meet with her and test her intentions.

So it was a fucking trap. The questions coursed through her brain. "What do I do?" she asked herself. "Should I wait? Forget about Duverger's file? I've got more important things to do—that's for sure. But who can help me investigate the sculptures? I've overestimated Gaudin. No point in turning to Mom. Should I even tell her about Magni's death? What about his ex-mistress? No, she disappeared without leaving an address. Duverger is my only lead."

the piece—perhaps restorations that no one else had noticed. The other bidders were paralyzed, and before they could pull themselves together, the gavel dropped.

The room was buzzing now. The auctioneer carried the precious mask to the back of the room. The appraiser, his arms crossed, was leaning against the wall. He towered over everyone around him. With a subtle nod, he accepted the piece.

"Congratulations. That was an impressive win." Marion held out her hand and introduced herself.

She had been sitting not too far from him the whole time and watching him work his magic. The night before, she had started to pick up the phone several times before finally making the call. His file was missing the receipt and certificate of authenticity for the stolen shaman, so she had a valid reason to meet with him. Without even asking why she was calling, he proposed that they meet at the auction house. He gave her a detailed description of himself so she would be able to observe him. "It should be very suspenseful," he had told her.

The appraiser had gray eyes flecked with green. He looked her over for a moment, as if he needed time to place who she was, and then he leaned in and whispered, "Did you see that? So easy, right? You just slip a bit of doubt into the minds of your opponents, and they forfeit the game."

"Sure, but play that trick one too many times, and everyone will be wise to you," Marion answered. "I'm curious. Why did you reveal yourself? You could have done your bidding anonymously."

"It's Marion, right? Look at them..." Duverger directed her attention to the new round of bidding. "I could play them a hundred times, and they'd waver every time. Come on. Let's get out of here."

Indifferent to the many eyes on him, he took Marion's elbow and led her out of the room, down two flights of stairs, through a crowd of walk-ins, curiosity seekers, and potential bidders, and out of the building. A Bentley, its engine running, was waiting on the Rue de Drouot. Duverger opened the back door.

"Where are we going?" Marion asked, stopping cold.

"My office."

She hesitated, looked around the busy street, jumped at a car honking, and slipped into the backseat.

Sitting next to her, Duverger propped his elbow on the armrest. His eyes were fixed on the back of the chauffeur's head. Marion thought he looked tense and distracted. The man also looked tired. He had a five o'clock shadow.

She watched as Duverger took out a sterling silver cigarette case with emerald cabochons. A leather jacket, gems, jeans, an expensive limo... He clearly stood out in the prissy and uptight world of art collectors and appraisers.

He lit a cigarette without asking if it bothered her. She searched the back of the limo for something to focus on. Her eyes landed on the mask. The piece that Duverger had just paid nearly two hundred thousand euros for was lying next to his foot. One careless move, and it would be as worthless as a kid's party mask. She couldn't believe his indifference. He stretched out his legs and turned toward her with feline flexibility.

"So, you wanted to speak with me?"

"You're the one who contacted us."

"I'm all ears," he replied, amused. "What would you like to know?"

"There's no certificate of authenticity in the file you gave us."

"You didn't ask for it."

"Do you have it?"

"I bought that shaman sculpture for an American collector. At two hundred thirty thousand euros you're allowed to call the shots."

"There's no receipt in your file either."

"That's not surprising. I don't have one. It was an off-the-books transaction."

She thought for a moment.

"Is that a problem?" he asked.

"With the receipt? No. But I'm a little confused."

"Why's that?"

"I've seen a piece that's pretty similar to this one..." She hesitated before going for it. She didn't know where it would lead, but she couldn't think of a better way. "I saw it at Edmond Magni's estate."

"At Edmond Magni's estate," the appraiser repeated. He observed her for a few seconds.

He could have expressed his surprise and said something about the strange coincidence. But instead he responded, "You're lucky you got to visit his home. Very few have been invited into his pantheon. I only got as far as his parlor and didn't get to see any of his sculptures. How did you—"

"But you're familiar with some of them," she interrupted to avoid further explanation. "He was one of your clients."

"Yes... Until about four years ago, when he cut all ties. It was right after a dinner party at his place. Probably the only one he hosted in his life. A hard thing to forget! I never saw him after that."

That meant Duverger couldn't have sold the pieces to her father, and there was no Studio 6 connection.

So what about the stolen shaman? Maybe the case wasn't a ruse. And yet something bothered her. This appraiser wasn't someone who would waste his time with a lowly employee of an outfit like SearchArt. He could have dealt with her and the missing documents back at the auction house. What did he want?

"We're here. Are you coming?" he asked, opening the door of the limo.

The car ride had lasted only a few minutes. They were just a few blocks from Hôtel Drouot, in front of a decrepit building with a chipped wrought-iron door and a façade streaked with pigeon droppings. What a cliché. Marion knew many appraisers and collectors who had offices in worse-for-the-wear buildings, as if the contrast highlighted the prestige of the professions.

Marion followed Duverger past the out-of-commission elevator and up an old staircase with a wobbly railing. Arriving on the right floor, Duverger ushered her to a heavy door that led to another heavy door, neither of which had a working security pad. The second door opened to a pathetic room that appeared to serve as a reception area. There was a melamine table with two chairs, and on it were auction catalogs. They were chained to the wall. Look but don't touch. Cheapskates.

"This way," Duverger said, directing her toward a larger room. "Let's have a drink here. It's nice and quiet. No one comes in on Saturday. Please, make yourself comfortable."

Marion didn't know if she should be relieved or worried by his informality. She sat down on a bar stool that he had pulled from under a large oak workbench, which was strewn with optical instruments.

This strange space was a cross between an artist's studio and an Arab market. She was surrounded by rolled-up carpets, ewers, bronze statues, warrior vases, and terra-cotta religious figures. Most of them were lying on the floor—priceless pieces treated like so much junk. Only a buyer could commit such sacrilege.

Against the walls, large display cabinets stretched from the floor to the ceiling. They were filled with precious objects. She noted Fabergé eggs, quartz axes, jade bowls, and emerald necklaces, none of which she would have expected from an expert in pre-Columbian art.

Just as she was about to get up and examine the treasures, Marion heard a loud clatter. She looked toward the noise and saw Duverger shutting the blinds. The room turned pitch black. Not a single trace of light was able to seep through.

Startled, Marion was trying to get her bearings when she heard the appraiser walking toward her. She froze, not daring to turn around. He slowly brushed her back, then moved away. Was he holding something? Scissors, a knife, keys? The room was so silent, she could hear the ringing in her ears. Then she heard a click, and Duverger's face was lit in the beam of an anglepoise lamp, which made his five o'clock shadow look criminal-like and his eyes beady. He adjusted the angle of the lamp.

"Vodka, bourbon?"

Marion didn't respond. Her nerves were as taut as violin strings. Why had he closed the blinds in the middle of the day?

"I also have sparkling water and cola, if you prefer," he pressed.

"Sparkling water please..."

Her voice drifted off. She watched the appraiser's shadow on the ceiling lengthen as he walked toward a small refrigerator. He took out two bottles and started back, his shadow shortening to human size the closer he got. Finally, he sat down across from her, reached down, and pulled up his newly acquired mask. He set it atop the workbench, directly under the lamp.

"This is how Magni said an object should be assessed once the love-at-first-sight feeling passed," he said, gazing at the mask. "I haven't found a better system. He'd make the room pitch black, with the exception of a single spotlight, to eliminate all distractions. If the piece was able to captivate him for several hours, his decision was made. It would stay by his side, his sole selection, while he waited for something better. But if it failed to sustain his interest, it would go in the closet. In his cellar, I'm assuming. I don't know where he hid his collection. And yet I really thought," he continued pensively, "that he was planning to show us. I seriously believed that was why he organized the dinner."

Twice now Duverger had brought up the dinner, as if he was expecting Marion to pursue the subject. She decided to follow his lead.

"Which dinner?"

"Do you have time to hear the whole story? Because once I get started..." He was still staring at the mask.

She nodded, even though she had the distinct feeling that she was being steered out to sea by a crazed captain. Even more ludicrous, Duverger appeared to be talking to the mask, not her. His mimicking of Magni's methodology bordered on absurd.

"There were fifteen of us," Duverger said. "Magni had brought together the biggest names in the art world: historians, auctioneers, and antiques dealers. All of us shared an interest in pre-Columbian art, and we knew one another, by name at least..."

Duverger continued to observe the mask as he went on. "Think about it. One of the world's most famous art collectors had invited us to his private mansion. A privilege that, up until this night, hadn't been granted to anyone else. Everyone was dressed to the nines. But guess how he greeted us. Like Hugh Hefner. In a dressing gown. But this was no ordinary dressing gown. It was Persian silk. And on his feet were oriental slippers. What an impression he made. He was wearing a heavy vetiver fragrance. His hair was slicked back. And even I noticed his eyes. They were a true green with thick black lashes. He cut quite a figure. He was a Persian prince straight out of Scheherazade. All that was missing were the eunuchs. But I'm getting ahead of myself. Just imagine the expressions on the faces of the stuck-up guests squeezed into their tuxes and sequin dresses."

Marion had no problem picturing the scene.

"They were all trying desperately to keep their cool and act as though nothing was strange. I'm sure they wanted their host to believe that nothing could shock them. After all, Magni did have a reputation of being a bit of a kook. I wondered what he had in store for us. The parlor décor was overstated, to say the least. Venetian mirrors hung all over the walls. Some of them were opposite each other, so it was easy to lose perspective. Dozens of candelabras accentuated the otherworldly feel. A table in the middle of the room was loaded with silver and orange peonies. In the corners there were Greco-Roman statues made of pink-veined marble and life-size lions with gaping mouths. The ambiance was very strange. Very eccentric."

Marion shifted and rubbed her hands together.

"We settled down little by little, and the conversation picked up a rhythm. Eventually we started talking about pre-Columbian art. I can still hear Joseph Chartier, the socialite and historian. I'm sure you've heard of him."

Marion couldn't believe how a piece of art could hold anyone's attention this long. Her mother was capable of staring at a painting for a long time, but it was nothing compared with this. Sooner or later, Duverger had to look away from the mask.

"Anyway, Chartier was all about pre-Columbian art that night—I'd say even more than the rest of us. Mind you, one-on-one, he was a sharp and insightful guy. He could tell terrific stories. But on this night, he was full of clichés and had nothing but derision for so-called art experts who never gave these Latin American pieces their due. He was prattling on and on. And he was going at it with that parvenu Alain Ozenberg, a Parisian dealer—one of the biggest in pre-Columbian art. Nobody likes Ozenberg—he's too good-looking and too successful."

Duverger tilted his head slightly to get a new perspective on the mask.

"Anyway, that's when Magni stood up. 'The greatest art, the only art, is fucking!' he declared, raising his glass of 1929 Romanée-Conti. There he was, the renowned art collector, standing at the head of the table with his dressing gown open, giving everyone a full view of his pecs, which were actually well defined, now that I look back on it. I can tell you, the silence at that table was heavy. None of us knew how to react. You can imagine the look of fear on some of the faces."

Duverger paused for a minute—a very long minute for Marion.

"'Fucking calls on every sense, every emotion,' Magni continued, looking each of us in the eye. 'The smells, the sounds, the touch, the taste, the sight, the lust, the creativity. What other art form is more complete? Hell, after one good fuck you can't wait to get your mojo back to go at it again. When was the last time you felt that way about a statue or a painting?'

"The woman next to me almost choked on her *magret de canard*. You'll never guess who it was: Françoise Vigan."

La Medici? What was she doing there? Sure, her boss was a great schmoozer, but Marion had a hard time imagining Magni putting her on par with all those major players and granting her a spot at his dinner table.

"As always, she was wearing black—a lace dress. It looked great on her, by the way. That's one woman who doesn't get thrown off easily. Am I right? But she was as white as a sheet and sweating."

Marion was getting annoyed. Duverger was trying to mess with her. And he still hadn't taken his eyes off the mask.

"I wanted to applaud him. Yes, he was considered an eccentric, but Magni was also shrewd, cold, relentless, and cruel. He stared at us with a victorious look on his face, while we glared back with suspicion. You see, we were prisoners of convention. A glimmer of compassion flashed in his eyes before he snapped his fingers and introduced the second act of his little farce."

Marion stood up and started pacing. Last week she was an ordinary woman going about her ordinary life—not the daughter of a larger-than-life... What? A larger-than-life what? A number of contradicting answers to that question ran through her head.

Duverger didn't seem to take notice of her agitation and continued his tale.

"Two women emerged from behind a silk wall hanging at the back of the room. Their bodies were tight and muscular, and their bronze skin was sprinkled with gold dust. They wore gauzy white veils, gold hammered cuffs around their necks, nariguera nose rings, and dangling earrings. They were beautiful: almond eyes, high cheekbones, and long black hair with cinnamon highlights.

"I was mesmerized, and I wasn't the only one. I had never seen such splendid creatures. They looked like Huastec goddesses of fertility. Or rather, given the circumstances, Inca virgins that the cacique nobles and priests offered Inti, the sun god. Because, right then and there, Magni was going to sacrifice them himself!

"He swept everything in front of him off the table. He took one of the young women by the arm and laid her out. He slowly slipped his hands up her gold-sequin cloak until he reached her breasts. I glimpsed an emerald in her navel. It looked like a cat's eye."

Marion took note: an emerald.

"As beautiful as the girl was, I was fascinated with the stone," the appraiser continued. "It was gorgeous, perfectly round, like a marble. Not a single flaw. Nature's mastery at work. It was a translucent greenish-blue. I hadn't seen this color in a very long time."

Marion looked up instinctively in search of the jewels she had spotted in the cabinets. But the room was too dark.

"Then Magni spread her legs and opened his robe all the way. I closed my eyes. It was more than even I could handle. One after another, we stood up and got out of there. I was the last to leave. When I reached the door, I turned and saw that he was back in his chair, an arrogant smile on his face. The two majestic women were standing behind him. I pitied him."

"You pitied him?" Marion said. "After such a display? You should have loathed him!"

"You couldn't," Duverger replied coolly. "He was a genius, a man with a sharp eye and an instinct that never failed. I watched his performances at the auction houses countless times. He'd stand in the doorway for a brief moment and get a feel for the room. And without fail, he'd walk right up to the most interesting object on display. He didn't need a catalog, a certificate of analysis, or expert advice. He just knew how to read a piece. In a glance, he could tell exactly where it came from and exactly how it was used."

Listening to Duverger, Marion realized that Bruno had been right. Magni was such a paragon, no one—not even this well-known appraiser—questioned his brilliance. As far as she was concerned, though, there was something exaggerated and ridiculous about the way people idolized him.

"He was intuitive and inspired," Duverger continued. "And he eschewed civility and pretense. He was trying to tell us that our gut instincts and senses are just as important—if not more important—than our degrees. His message was intended for the curators who are uninformed about what they have in their museums, the people who call themselves experts because they've gone to the right school, and the gallery owners who run trendy businesses just so they can socialize with the big names. The problem with Magni was that his message got lost in the delivery. And that's what happened. The day after the dinner, the only thing people were wondering was whether he actually fucked those women. They didn't give a shit about what he was actually saying."

Marion didn't know what to think. What Duverger was telling her made no sense to her.

"What good is it being a master if you don't have followers?" she eventually asked. "Magni knew that hardly anyone would get his point."

"I thought the same thing at first, but I was wrong. He made his own rules. He wasn't concerned with morals or conventions. He was a free agent who found animosity easier to deal with than admiration if it was coming from people or institutions that he didn't like. He actually took joy in inspiring scorn. That's exactly what made him free. He had no followers, no expectations, no fear."

Marion was baffled. The more information she took in, the more confused she became. What was she to make of this man whose cellar was full of centuries-old figures with hollow eyes and oversized genitals? A man who'd invite important people to his home and then proceed to have sex in front of them. But also an intellectual tyrant who dictated what others should believe and had absolute conviction in the correctness of his own opinions.

"You seem distracted."

"It's just that your description of my…"

"My?" the broker repeated.

She looked up and, after making unexpected eye contact with Duverger, felt the blood rising like a schoolgirl with a flushed face.

"My client. Magni entrusted us with a file just before he died," she said, immediately regretting the cover-up. He'd have no trouble finding out that this was a lie if he talked to La Medici.

"Ah," Duverger replied, sounding unconvinced by her evasive response. "That would explain why you saw my shaman at his home."

And they had come full circle. She doubted that Duverger had brought her to his office just to tell her stories about Magni and his high jinks. Was he waiting for her to trip up and using this time to observe her?

"And what if the shaman that was stolen from me is actually at his place?" Duverger asked.

Marion didn't know how to answer. "What would it be doing there?" she was barely able to muster.

"That's what I'm hoping you'll tell me..."

4

Her thoughts racing, Marion threw off her coat. "He knows. He knows I'm Magni's daughter. That auctioneer who called me, Mr. Rambert, figured it out. Why wouldn't Duverger? The case he brought us could be a complete lie. Was La Medici in cahoots with him?" She bent down to unlace her ankle boots. "That means the shaman may not have been stolen. But why would it be at my dad's house?" She took off her turtleneck and wiggled out of her pants. "What's his game plan? Why didn't he put all his cards on the table at the start?" She stuffed her bra and panties into her bag and slipped into her bathing suit. "And that dinner... Why did he tell me all about Magni's creepy behavior in full detail?" Marion grabbed her towel and jetted out of the changing room.

The inner dialogue continued. "Magni throws a party at his place for the first time in his life, and it becomes a scandal, perfectly planned and orchestrated." She instinctively handed her things to a sixty-year-old rocker planted behind the counter. "What was on his mind?" She slipped on a yellow plastic bracelet bearing her locker number. "The dinner, then, a few months later, the auction." An old black wall phone started ringing. "Magni becomes even more reclusive. Won't appear in public, won't sell..." Carried by the King's voice on the radio, Marion rushed toward the pool.

Swimming laps was Marion's stress reliever and her means of escape.

The pool was practically empty. It was always empty, actually. Only twenty-five meters long, it wasn't big enough for competitive athletes and not hip enough for cool kids. But it was charming, with its Art Nouveau columns and sage-green ceramic tiles with lotus details.

Behind her goggles, which gave the pool lights a bluish tint, Marion was starting to feel looser and stronger. Only her neck was still holding some tension, but it soon succumbed to the rhythm of her strokes. She thought again about Duverger's innuendos and subtle approach. The appraiser was sneaky, adept at scheming and manipulating. "My exact opposite," she said to herself as she started her fifth lap.

"Life is a chess game." Peter—her ex—loved that cliché. Incapable of anticipating her opponent's moves, she greedily gobbled his pieces, not realizing that they could be sacrificed until after she had placed her stakes elsewhere.

Ten feet below and on the left side of the pool, two scuba divers, with fins on their feet, oxygen tanks on their backs, and masks covering half their faces, were sealing cracks in the tiles. They looked like a couple of sea mammals as they worked their way from one tiny fissure to another.

Marion had been swimming for a while now, and she was no longer thinking about Duverger. She had her rhythm and was absorbed in the act of stroking and breathing. One kilometer down… She was tired, but that wouldn't stop her. The hands on the wall clock pointed to four thirty. Just below it was the lifeguard, his nose deep in a newspaper. She glanced from time to time at the divers sharing the pool with her.

She focused on her crawl. It was becoming slower with each stroke. As she neared the spot where she had seen the divers on her last lap, she noticed that they were gone. They didn't stay very long. She looked around the pool between breaths, trying to spot them. Distracted, she lost her rhythm. She kicked to regain speed and inadvertently swallowed water. She started choking. Now her strokes were all off. Her goggles had become a nuisance. They had fogged up.

Marion stopped at the end of the pool to catch her breath. Her lungs were barely replenished when she felt someone wrap his hands around her ankles and pull her down. Someone was yanking her toward the bottom. She clutched the side of the pool with all her might, but she lost her grip, and her head went under. Frantic, she tried to claw her way to the surface. Where was the lifeguard?

She looked down, powerless. The two divers were latched onto her ankles and looking up at her. Their large eyes bulged behind the deforming lenses of their masks. She fought. After a few seconds, the desire to surrender washed over her. But a voice screamed in her head. "Don't give up!"

Anger, aggression, and survival instinct gave her a final burst of energy. She jerked her right leg free. But the hold on her other ankle tightened. She was being pulled deeper into the abyss. There was no air left in her lungs. The water blocked all ways out. Blood rushed to her head, and her eyes rolled back. Her mouth filled with water. Marion sank like a dead weight.

~ ~ ~

She heard voices. A door closed softly. Someone took a seat beside her. She wanted to keep her eyes shut. Her heart was beating wildly. She felt wound up like a cuckoo clock. She was scared. What had happened? Marion pictured the two twisted faces, their features distorted by their masks. Did those guys want her dead? Just thinking about it made her shiver. She wanted to go to sleep and forget about it. She was exhausted. Her body was as floppy as a rag doll.

She cracked one eye open anyway. Then closed it just as quickly. It was her mother. She was easily the last person Marion wanted to see. The woman's manic depression was more than she could handle at the moment. Marion peeked again. Yep, the woman staring at her was definitely her mother. Usually her pupils were fixed and dilated, a symptom of her self-absorption. But now she was giving Marion a harsh look. "Probably because she had to think of me for once, instead of herself," Marion thought.

Marion couldn't fake sleep much longer. Her mother was making her too uncomfortable. She opened her eyes and glanced around the white room humming with fluorescent lights.

"Honey!"

Her mother's freckled face, framed by brown curls, lit up. She smiled at her and moved closer.

"Finally! I was afraid you weren't going to wake up until after I left. I know, I know. I'm sorry, I can't stay long. You look great, though. They got me all worried. They told me you almost drowned. But I said it had to be a joke. I told them how you swim like a fish. Turns out I was right. It wasn't that bad. You just swallowed a little water. I had to take a sedative to calm down. You know how I feel about hospitals. But seriously, I've got to head back home. I lost my watch."

Her hands were flying around like crazed birds.

"I've been without that watch for two days now. It's ridiculous. I looked everywhere. Giselle says I threw it out the window. But I think she stole it. I—"

"Okay, Mom, okay!" Marion cried out. Her mother's incoherent rambling was already wearing her down. "I'm fine. You can leave if you want to."

"You know, without my watch I don't know when to take my pills. They upped me to twenty a day. I have to take them at just the right time, or else it'll start up again!"

"I'd lend you one, but I don't wear a watch."

"I know. I looked in your bag. I thought mine might be in there. You could have borrowed it."

"But I haven't seen you in weeks."

"What if it was in your bag, and that nurse stole it?"

"What nurse?"

"The one I saw earlier."

"Mom. Go home. I'm sure Giselle has found it by now."

Marion couldn't think of anything else to say to make her leave. She was worried that her mother would have an episode right there in her room. The various drugs the woman took subdued her temper but not her obsessive thoughts. And her moods turned so quickly, it was impossible to predict when another fit of hysteria would occur.

When her irrational imaginings broke through the logic barrier, she'd sometimes become a soldier ready to save the world from the invisible threat—whatever that was. The hot-water kettle would start revving like an army tank. The bedside lamp would become a bomb. The bread knife would be her machine gun.

All she needed was the signal, and she'd be off—a twenty-first-century Joan of Arc.

The door of her room cracked open, and a face peeped through the opening. It was a much welcome face with coarse stubble. The bags under his hazel eyes accentuated a look of fatigue.

"Is it okay if I join you?"

"Chris!" Marion sat up and beamed at her friend. "I'm so happy to see you."

"Your mother called as soon as she found out that you were in the emergency room. I've been waiting for you to wake up."

Marion looked at her mother. Pretending to ignore Marion, she hastened to put on a pair of gray gloves and picked up her purse.

"I'm getting you out of here," Chris said. Marion blinked. His lanky body seemed to be floating. "The doctors say everything's fine. Low blood sugar. You just got dizzy and passed out."

"Dizzy? What are you talking about? They wanted to—"

Marion stopped short. Her mother had stealthily taken her hand.

"I'd love to take you home and look after you, but you know I can't. I just have too much on my mind. Would you call Giselle and make sure she has my watch?"

"Yes, I promise I'll call her as soon as I'm back at my apartment."

Once she was gone, Marion covered her face with her hand.

"I couldn't tell her about Magni."

"In her mind, he's been dead a long time," Chris said.

Chris was the only person Marion could count on. He was just as much a loner as she was, and he understood how she valued her privacy, because he valued his. They had met twelve years earlier at the École du Louvre and had become close friends thanks to heated arguments they would have about antiques, the nature of beauty, and people's fascination with art.

"Okay, let's go. Get dressed," he instructed as he pulled her clothes out of the closet and handed them to her. "I'm taking you out to dinner. How does prime rib sound? It's all I can think about. I'm starving."

Chris helped Marion get up and turned his back while she dressed. She felt weak and empty. Her hands were trembling like leaves in the wind. With her clothes on at last, she sat down on the bed. She was too tired and anxious to face the world.

"Are you okay, Marion? Should I call the nurse?"

"I think someone wants me dead."

"What?"

"In the pool. Two guys tried to drown me."

Chris flashed a dubious look before sitting down next to her.

"But the doctors said—"

"They don't know what happened. They only know that somebody fished me out of the pool and called the paramedics."

"Maybe it was just some kids who were messing around. They were teasing you, and it went too far."

"If they were kids, they were well-trained kids. And strong. I'm telling you, these guys planned their attack! They took their time and waited until just the right moment, probably when the lifeguard was taking a break."

"If they wanted to eliminate you, they'd have done it."

"Something—or someone—stopped them."

"And how could they have gotten away?"

"You don't believe me!"

"Of course I do, but maybe you're exaggerating a bit. You've been through a lot."

"Maybe they were just trying to scare me."

"Why would they want to do that?"

"Maybe they were warning me to give up my search for the sculptures."

"Who's they? No one's supposed to know about you. Isn't that right? The estate attorney promised to keep everything confidential. I haven't told anyone. Who could possibly want to hurt you? You're blowing this entirely out of proportion, Marion."

"Gaudin knows."

As soon as his name left her mouth, her suspicions about the man seemed too obvious to be true.

"And maybe Duverger, La Medici, and Rambert. I don't care what the estate attorney said. You know how the art world works. Artworks may get stolen and stay under wraps for years, but secrets are traded out in the open. I'm almost positive they all know I'm Magni's daughter. They may even have more information than that. Enough to eliminate me from the picture."

"Duverger? Rambert? Who are they? Whatever... You're being paranoid. As big a name as Magni was, the whole world didn't revolve around him."

"Never mind," Marion muttered. Chris didn't know all the facts and couldn't possibly assess the situation.

An awkward silence settled in the room.

"Okay, let's say you're right," Chris finally said. "What do we do now?"

Marion shrugged. She was too overwhelmed to make any decisions. She was having a hard time holding back her tears, but she didn't want to break down in front of Chris. He would feel awkward about consoling her, especially now that he was married—to a real nut job, in Marion's opinion. At least his wife wasn't the jealous type, or she would have lost his friendship long ago.

"Come on. Let's get that food," he insisted. "It'll take your mind off things."

Nope, nothing could take her mind off this, but she wanted company.

She got up with immense effort just as a nurse entered the room and handed her an envelope.

"This was left for you at the reception desk."

Marion looked at Chris for a second and then anxiously unfolded a piece of paper. On it were three words in flawless, rounded cursive: "Watch your back."

5

Visions of masked snorkelers kept her thrashing in her bed until she realized that trying to sleep was useless.

She stumbled across her loft studio—in a converted hosiery factory–and ran into a pile of books.

"Shit."

Her bed faced a fireplace with just a mirror on the mantel. Marion looked at her reflection. Her eyes were red from crying. Under them were dark blue circles.

At the other end of the room were two leather armchairs, a cream-colored couch, a glass coffee table, and a potted palm tree. It was all the furniture she would allow in her home after spending her days surrounded by artwork. The minimalist look complemented the old bricks and industrial metal.

In the kitchenette, Marion forgot to fill the coffeemaker with water before turning it on.

"Dammit."

Her brain wasn't engaged. She'd forgo the caffeine. After pouring some tap water in a mug, she flopped into one of the leather chairs.

Marion was strung out. Chris had stayed too long the previous night. He thought conversation would help her sleep better. So she filled him in on the day's developments.

"Chris, I'm scared now," she had told him. "The pool is my place. That's where I unwind, my haven.

Why'd they have to strike there? Why not outside my office, or even here?"

"Marion, you're making too much of this. There's no 'they.' Put it behind you and move on."

"Admit it, Chris. My life has gotten a bit complicated since the estate lawyer called. But why? My father wasn't trying to compensate for his absence. No, he had other things in mind."

"Paranoia isn't going to help."

"I can't believe Magni didn't know the whereabouts of the sculptures when he wrote his will. Those were the only pieces he ever sold, according to Gaudin. Why didn't he leave any clues? Maybe it was his eccentric way of testing my determination."

At that point, Chris had started looking at his watch.

"Do you need to get back to your lady love?" Marion asked.

Chris frowned and looked away. "Don't change the subject, Marion. Your father didn't want anything to do with you when you were growing up, so such an elaborate plan focused on you seems a bit of a stretch. Maybe he just didn't have anyone else to give the collection to. End of story."

"Still, he's six feet under, and he's calling the shots. I don't like being steered by a dead man, even if it is my father."

"Well, if you want my honest opinion, I think you're just freaking out because you have to deal with power struggles and people crawling out of the woodwork—Gaudin, Duverger, and God knows who else. You hate confrontation. In fact, you do your best to avoid emotional involvement. Look at the boyfriends you choose so analytically."

She had stood up then and starting puttering in the kitchenette, with her back turned to him. He wasn't entirely wrong. "There are fewer disruptions that way," she said.

"Too bad about that last one," Chris threw in.

"Peter?"

"You know he really cared about you."

"He was insufferable. Too cloying."

"Cloying. That's what you call it? I call it affection when a guy shows up at his girl's door to steal her away from her books and take her to a concert, especially when it's not even the music that he likes. Remember that big house party he threw?"

"Yeah, he arrived early to pick me up. I hate surprises. And I hate crowds."

Marion had no desire to socialize or be seen by others. And now, ironically, she seemed to be the focus of a great deal of attention, and as much as Chris wanted her to put the whole thing out of her mind, she couldn't.

~ ~ ~

After calling in sick, Marion had gone back to bed. Now, she was up again and drumming the armrest of her chair. Chris had promised to swing by today. She checked the position of the sun in the window and surmised that it was well into the afternoon. Where was he? Just then, she heard banging at the door. Marion got up to answer, and Chris raced in without giving Marion a second look. Still wearing his coat, he threw himself into one of the armchairs.

"What a day!"

"What time is it?" she asked.

"Four thirty, maybe later..."

"You took your sweet time," she replied.

"I was at work, Marion, and I see that you weren't."

"I had an excuse."

"Well, I did not, and I couldn't get here any earlier. My boss left five messages on my cell last night. He wanted me at the lab at eight o'clock sharp."

Chris analyzed and authenticated antiques for a private lab.

"It's not your habit to respond to other people's emergencies, Chris."

"Except yours, of course."

"You could have called me," Marion said, wondering whether Chris would get around to asking her how she was doing.

"I was waiting for confirmation on a few things that may interest you."

"What?"

"It's about Chartier, the historian—you know, that socialite dandy who's all over the media."

Marion perked up. Laurent Duverger had mentioned Chartier as one of the guests at Magni's dinner party.

"When I showed up at the office, who did I find? Didier Combes."

"What was our favorite white-collar crimes detective doing there?" Combes headed up the art theft division of the Banditry Repression Brigade.

"He was looking for information about a pre-Columbian sculpture that belonged to Chartier—a Peruvian warrior."

Marion's heart was racing. Did Chartier have one of her sculptures?

"We were able to dig up a couple of X-rays taken in our lab, plus an authentication analysis, but it wasn't very thorough. He wanted anything that we might have: photos, analyses, the certificate, the whole shebang."

"And?" she asked, hanging onto his every word.

"Nothing, unfortunately. We searched through all our archives—they're a huge mess now that Michel's gone. You'd think he took off with some of our files."

"Michel's the one you fired?"

"Yeah..."

"Why was Combes looking for these documents?"

"I'm assuming Chartier got robbed. I couldn't get anything out of the detective. You know Combes isn't a very talkative one."

She certainly did. The first Thursday of every month, she would meet Combes for lunch to go over their casework. He was the only detective she met this way. With the others, she talked on the phone or corresponded via e-mail. But Combes was an old-timer who preferred to deal with people face-to-face. He prided himself on using his street smarts, not modern technology, to solve his cases.

Marion stared at the floor.

"Do you think it's one of yours?" Chris asked.

"I need to find a woman with child, a jaguar, and a warrior, so maybe. But there are thousands of warrior sculptures. We need a more detailed description."

"It's pretty weird, though. A bit of a coincidence, wouldn't you say?"

"The warrior I'm looking for has geometric designs on the right side and emerald inlays. Is there any chance at all that you could find a photo?"

"A photo..." Chris slapped his forehead. "Jesus Christ. I'm such an idiot. Why didn't I think of it? You've got the pictures of your pieces, don't you?"

Marion nodded.

"Give them to me. I'll see what I can find tomorrow. It could very well be that we handled the warrior while your father owned it. If that's the case, we should be able to make a match, based on what we already have and your photos. We'll get the certificate of authenticity and the name of the most recent owner, and that'll be it. Who knows, we might be able to find a match for more than one of the sculptures."

"But you can't even find a file for Chartier," Marion responded listlessly.

"The problem with Chartier is that the X-rays and the analysis are all that our lab has to work with right now, thanks to Michel and his mismanagement. We have the same system that you guys have at SearchArt. We archive the files based on images and descriptions of the piece. With the pictures you give us, we might have enough. I can run them through photo recognition."

"It doesn't hurt to try, but there are a lot of labs like yours in France," Marion responded.

Chris pulled out his cell phone. "But our lab is the best, isn't it? Pieces of this caliber would have come to us."

"That's assuming they've been analyzed."

"It's worth a shot. Everyone wants certificates of authenticity, with all the counterfeits floating around these days." Chris looked at his phone. "Oh God, my boss has left a bunch more messages already." He brought the phone to his ear and whispered as he listened to the recordings. "They want me to come in at eight again tomorrow. The boss sounds furious. I don't—"

"That's exactly what I was afraid of. It must be complete chaos at your lab. Anyway, this is just a wild-goose chase arranged by some crazy old man who's now dead. This is not who I am, Chris. In fact, it's a perfect example of how art can make you nuts."

"Stop that, Marion. Get a grip! This is a once-in-a-lifetime experience. And you're about to be showered with millions! Think of it. Millions! Sure, this is a little scary, but don't the adventure and the money make it worthwhile?"

"I'll never be able to find the sculptures."

"Have more faith in yourself, Marion. I know you can do it."

"Look at me," she replied, getting closer to him. "What do you see in my eyes?"

He leaned in, half curious, half amused.

"Determination…"

"No, Chris. It's fear. Fear. And I can't shake it."

6

Chris left shortly afterward. He said he needed to appease his wife. Rummaging for something to eat, Marion wondered what else was wrong. To this point, Chris's wife hadn't minded the time he spent with her.

Before leaving, Chris had put his finger on her own problem: the millions.

The market was anticipating just one thing: that Marion would sell. A collection like this came along only once every couple of decades. Manna for the birds of prey. Unfathomable works of art—and lots of them. Astonishing pieces that would be sold and resold for years.

There was nothing in the refrigerator but a few eggs and a bottle of milk.

Why would he give all that to her? Maybe Chris was right. Maybe he just didn't have anyone else to give the collection to. End of story.

She opened the vegetable drawer. A limp carrot.

Except for Gaudin. He had to be brooding. He couldn't possibly understand the will's conditions—or fathom how he had gotten completely robbed. He had served the man for thirty years. He had indulged the man's obsessions, his desires, and his craziness as if they were his own. He wouldn't want her to sell. Would he be content to keep an eye on Marion until he learned her game plan? Or was he trying to hurt her? And did those three sculptures have something to do with it?

"He's the one." Marion almost yelled it. She couldn't see anyone else in the picture with enough motive.

She slammed the refrigerator door. "Dammit, he tried to kill me!"

She felt her muscles tighten and bile rise. She paced the room, kicking a pile of books. Then she pulled out her phone. Maybe Chris was right, and there was some determination in her.

"What the hell were you thinking, trying to drown me? I'm not some plaything. Did you want to scare me? Or kill me?"

Marion's hands were shaking. On the other end of the line, George Gaudin said nothing.

"You won't admit it, will you? You're just waiting to get your share. Do you honestly think I'm going to give up?"

"Mademoiselle, I don't know what you are talking about."

"Come on. Are you going to answer me or not? I've got friends in the police force."

"I have nothing to say. I don't have any idea what you're referring to. There's no point threatening me."

"It would be quite convenient for you if I were out of the picture."

"Everyone knows I'm attached to that collection. But you give me more credit than I deserve. I don't decide whether people live or die."

"You'll have to try harder than that. You're the only person who could be upset about the inheritance."

"Listen, young lady, as much as you want to blame me for whatever happened to you, I didn't lift a finger against you. That collection is my flesh and blood, my sweat and tears. I've sacrificed everything for it.

I've spent so many years living without the company of others. If something happens to you, I won't shed any tears. But I'm telling you this: messing with you would mess up my entire life's work. And that's not going to happen."

"Is that it? You've got nothing else to offer in your defense?" Marion said, losing steam. "I don't know—maybe an idea of someone else who'd be interested in eliminating me?"

"First you accuse me, and then you ask me to find the real culprit?" Gaudin was getting one up on her now, but something had softened in his voice. "Art aficionados all over the world were envious of that collection, and Magni had belittled so many experts and curators, any one of them could want to take their revenge. And any number of them would sell his soul in a minute to the highest bidder."

There was a long silence.

"Can you tell me more about the sculptures?" Marion finally asked, kicking herself for sounding like a frightened little girl.

"Yes, the sculptures. If you insist. The first one Magni brought back was the *Woman with Child*. An astonishing work. This was the most valuable piece in his collection. But the figure disappeared almost immediately. Then, in rapid succession, two similar pieces showed up—the warrior and the jaguar. I remember them vividly. Such priceless objects were usually buried deep in royal tombs. Magni, of course, supplied no explanation. He was rarely in Paris during that period, but was spending most of his time in Latin America, leaving me in charge of the collection. It wasn't until much later that I learned that the sculptures had been sold at auction."

7

Still groggy, Marion turned over in her bed and felt around for the phone.

"One of your sculptures—the woman with disproportionately sized ear lobes..."

It was Chris.

"What about it?" she replied softly, glancing at the clock.

"It was analyzed at our lab in July, right after your dad got rid of it. See, I was right to insist—"

"Are you calling from your office?"

"Where else would I be?"

"Do you know what time it is?"

"Seven thirty. I've been here all night—just for you."

"Or maybe just to avoid going home?"

"Marion, this isn't about me, okay? I'm telling you that I just found an owner. This is a lead—our only lead at the moment. I thought you'd be jumping for joy."

"Who does it belong to?" she finally asked.

Chris shuffled some papers. "Oh good, so you're awake now?"

"I'm awake."

"I thought you had more fight in you."

"Are you done lecturing me?"

"Alain Ozenberg. He's one of our best clients."

Marion was sitting up now. He was another one of the guests at the party.

"A big shot in pre-Columbian art. There's no way of knowing if he still has the sculpture, but at least we have something to work with. You should also know that he has a reputation. He's pushed through some questionable deals, and rumor has it he's stolen pieces from small Latin American museums. Some people even say he has a network of tomb raiders in Peru."

"Sounds like a solid lead. Maybe this one will pan out."

"What do you mean?"

Marion told him about her call to Gaudin the night before.

"Well, now we have Ozenberg, and I've got more on him. He's a player. Good looking. Before he became an art dealer he was a model and cover boy for *Vogue*. Take down this address: 64 Rue du Faubourg Saint-Honoré. You could probably stop by his gallery today. It's open."

"I don't have time."

"I wouldn't wait too long if I were you. The Munich Biennial Show starts in seven days, and you won't be able to reach him for two weeks."

Marion didn't say anything. She didn't feel brave enough or strong enough to deal with a stranger today.

"Hellooooo, is anyone there?"

"I was thinking."

"And?"

"I was planning to go to my dad's place today. I want to see if Duverger's sculpture is there."

A lie. She had nothing planned. She wanted to stay in her apartment behind a securely locked door, padding from the bed to the kitchenette and then to the sofa.

"I'll go with you."

"What?"

"I'll go to your dad's with you. I want to see the collection."

"But I thought your boss wanted you at the office."

"I'll make something up to get out of here."

"I don't know if that's a good idea." She needed to backtrack. "It might be a little tricky if we both go. What if we run into Gaudin?"

"I hope we do."

"I don't. I'm only going if he's not there."

"I know you, Marion. You've already figured out what time he leaves the house."

Marion felt trapped, and yet if she was going to make a decision it had to be now. Deep down she didn't hate the idea of having him by her side at her father's house. Even though her Gaudin-is-a-bad-guy theory was apparently a no-go, she was sure the man cared about his life's work being taken away from him.

She knew that Gaudin would be at the flea market, where once a week he spent the morning. He had told her this the first time they spoke, when she had asked him when it was best to call.

"I'll call you back," she finally said.

"No need. Let's just say we'll meet at your dad's in two hours. I'll keep my cell on in case there are any problems with Gaudin."

"Okay—but what about Ozenberg?" she blurted out.

"Why don't you do both today?"

"Can you come with me to see him too?"

"That's stretching it a bit. But I'll meet up with you afterward if you want."

~ ~ ~

From a bench in a small park, Marion was observing Magni's mansion just across the street. Where was Chris? Ever since leaving her place, she was sure she was being followed. Was it just stress? Marion had done a thorough survey of her surroundings. There was nothing suspicious or troubling. If anyone appeared borderline sketchy, it was she. A woman sweeping the sidewalk in front of the post-Haussmann-style building was staring at her. Here in Passy—a neighborhood of luxury apartments, few shops, public gardens, and no movie theaters—the slightest sign of something unusual could seem shady.

Bothered by the pair of eyes directed at her, Marion finally opted to get off the bench. She purposefully walked across the street and dashed toward the building, her head spinning from the split-second decision.

She unlocked the door with the key Gaudin had given her and slipped into the apartment. She leaned against a wall of the large parlor to regain her bearings. As her composure returned, she let the beauty of the space wash over her. Stucco and wood—very popular in the nineteenth century. She hadn't noticed it during her first visit, but from where she was standing now, she admired every chair, the big parquet table, the paintings—each angled toward a single vanishing point—and an ebony cabinet perched on Corinthian columns. It was a remarkable piece inlaid with baskets and birds of amethyst, agate, and mottled jasper.

There were no magazines, books, files, or pieces of mail. The parlor's sole purpose was displaying the antiques and art the owner of the mansion had collected, especially the cabinet. As she examined the space more closely, she saw that each object had been given a specific and permanent place. No room for nonessentials, whims, or fancies. She was about to go into the office when the abrasively loud doorbell interrupted her. Chris, smiling wildly—devilishly even—swept in and kissed her on the cheeks.

"Nice outfit," he said with a wink. "You're not really going to wear old jeans, a baggy top, and flats when you hit on Ozenberg, are you?"

"Don't start," she said, turning her back to him.

"I've never seen anything like this," Chris said. "He arranged his furniture and everything else perfectly. I'm getting chills. Everything's so beautiful."

"Magni surrounded himself with priceless objects as though they were a sort of shield. Wait till you see the cellar."

"Are you going to inherit all this too?" Chris caressed the wood of a Mazarin bureau and then carefully opened a drawer.

"Chris! You shouldn't—"

"There're aren't any papers anywhere," he said, ignoring her. "I wonder where he kept all his mail. Come on. Let's go upstairs. We have time, don't we? When will Gaudin be back?"

"Normally he spends the morning at the flea market, so I can't imagine he'll be back right away. I don't want to loiter too long, though."

"So we have five minutes to spare. Let's go!"

Chris grabbed her hand, clearly giddy.

One floor up, they roamed from room to room. As Marion went from one space to the next, she realized something: there were no clocks of any kind.

She walked over to one of the double-pane windows flanked by drapes as heavy as Doric columns. The window was wide and tall, a feature that made the building look larger from the outside. She glanced at the street, then turned back around. There was no tick-tocking, or any other noise, for that matter. No swoosh of a passing car, no creaky floorboards, no click of a furnace turning on.

"It's crazy," she said, sitting on the edge of a *lit à la polonaise*. "This place is a real tomb. Have you seen one TV or radio? Have you even spotted a CD player?"

"Silence is a luxury these days, like that bed you're sitting on was way back when. You know they call it a Polish bed because of King Louis XV's Polish queen, right? Of course you do," Chris said. He was opening and closing armoire doors and bureau drawers. "Check this out. Shirts, shirts, and more shirts. He had enough to wear a different one every day of the year. They're folded by color between sheets of tissue paper. Maybe I could hire his housekeeper. She'd do wonders for my place."

Marion started bouncing on the mattress—slowly at first, then more vigorously. "The mattress doesn't even make noise. Listen. Nothing." She looked under the box spring. Magni had reinforced the bed to keep it from squeaking. As she straightened up, a white splotch near the headboard caught her eye. She knelt next to the bedside table and reached for it. It was a crumpled piece of paper covered with a thin layer of dust. She smoothed it out. On it was a handwritten list of five items, with the first four crossed out:

~~*Woman with Child*~~
~~*Warrior*~~
~~*Crouched Figure Carrying the World*~~
~~*Jaguar*~~
Tattooed Man

It was a list of sculptures, including the three she had to find. But why were some crossed out? Did it mean they had been auctioned off? Or donated? And what were the crouched figure and the tattooed man? What were they doing on the list?

"Look at this." She held the paper in front of Chris, who was now sitting beside her.

"Where'd you find that?"

"Under the bed."

He ran his fingers over the dark blue ink. "This is the first piece of paper we've come across. And it's woven—classy stuff."

"It looks like someone meant to throw it out, then changed his mind."

"Gaudin?"

"Or Magni…"

"But if either of them wanted it, why was it lying crumpled next to the bed?"

Marion glanced around. "Who's room is this, anyway?" Like every other room in the house, the furniture was a barrier to any display of individuality. No pictures, no books—nothing that would give the space a unique identity.

"Chris, what size are the shirts?"

"XL. All of them. Too big for me. Otherwise I would've totally taken one. These threads are excellent."

"Gaudin looks like he's an XL. But for all I know, so was Magni." Marion sighed. "I was only three when my mother told me he was dead."

A loud slam disrupted the supernatural silence of the house. Marion and Chris looked at each other before the latter leaped up to close the bedroom door. They'd never make it as gumshoes. They scared too easily.

The apartment was quiet again. Without waiting any longer, Marion headed into the hallway, followed by Chris, and crept down the stairs. At the bottom, she peeked into the parlor. Seeing no one, the two of them hurried to the reinforced cellar door.

"There must be a draft somewhere in this place," Chris whispered.

Marion tried not to tremble as she fished out the two keys that opened the door. "I hope he gave me the real keys," she whispered. To her great relief, they fit the locks. After opening the door, Marion took a moment to absorb the darkness before fiddling with the lights.

At the bottom of the steps Marion pulled the photo of Laurent Duverger's shaman out of her bag. She handed the image to Chris, who stood motionless as he cast his eyes over the hundreds of otherworldly figures.

After a few minutes, he walked over to the closest display and started inspecting the figures. Marion thought he was the very picture of a Roman general inspecting the elite members of his Praetorian Guard. But despite the rigorous review, Chris found no match. The stone shaman in the image was upright, with crossed arms, a triangular face, and dark shadows where his eyes should have been. It had the alien look of a monumental Easter Island sculpture.

They moved on to another display. Chris hadn't opened his mouth or let out a single whistle of admiration. He looked overwhelmed. They moved from one exhibit to another. Still nothing. Then, just as she was about to give up, Marion glimpsed a spot that she hadn't seen before. And there he was, staring back at her. He was a bit off to the side, isolated from the others, radiating a sense of piousness and mystery.

"I was right," she said, reaching out to it.

"You've got a good eye. That's definitely it. What a beautiful piece."

Chris clapped with delight and spun around, almost losing his balance. Then he gasped. Marion looked to see what was the matter and stopped her hand midair when she saw Gaudin standing in the doorway, with his hands in his pockets and a scowl on his face.

"What are you doing here?"

The sound of Marion's voice seemed to get lost in the walls. It was Gaudin who had slammed the door and then crept up on them in this soundproofed vault.

"I could ask you the same thing. We don't have an appointment, as I recall."

Marion was determined not to let any of her trepidation show.

"We wanted to take a quick look at the collection by ourselves," she shot back with a smile. "This is my friend, Chris. Chris, Mr. Gaudin..."

Faced with his stubborn and suspicious silence, she continued. "There are so many pieces. Initially you don't see them as individual works, but instead as a collection. Then you begin to appreciate each one individually. This shaman, for example. I didn't notice it the other day. And yet it's so different from the others. Magni probably saw its unique features too, and that's why it was displayed a bit differently."

"If you look closely, there are similar shamans."

Marion searched for them. "Oh, there's an androgynous one." She approached the shelf where it was displayed. "You're right. I wasn't paying close enough attention."

"There are many more. Fifty-some in total. All made with impeccable craftsmanship," the assistant said at last. "It's a spectacular collection."

"Collection?"

Gaudin seemed to hesitate, and for a second Marion thought he would close up completely.

"A good number of years ago, your father met an old scholar, a former biology professor, Joseph Ernsen. The man was crazy about pre-Columbian art. But he had debts to pay off. Magni bought his collection cash on the barrel and preserved it until he died."

"What a nice gesture."

"A nice transaction," Gaudin corrected. "Your father was no philanthropist. He was betting on the man's addiction to gambling. He knew the fellow wouldn't give the cash to the people he owed money to. In fact, he gambled the money away and took on even more debt. He spent his final years chasing other pieces that he then sold to your father for a song—just to keep the loan sharks off his back. Your father did very well. He made a handsome profit on that man's vices."

Marion nodded distractedly. A typical dirty venture in capitalism. If he was telling the truth, what was Laurent Duverger's sculpture doing here? Because it no doubt belonged to him.

"But I know that shaman was stolen," she fired, fully prepared to grab the sculpture.

"Hands off!" Gaudin shouted, springing toward her.

Marion started and stepped back.

"Where did you hear that nonsense?" Gaudin asked.

"I have in my possession a perfectly legitimate declaration of theft."

"You have the wrong piece, then."

"The description is a perfect match. The photo too," Chris said, handing Gaudin the picture. "That shaman belongs to Laurent Duverger. He's the one who reported it stolen."

Marion hadn't taken her eyes off Gaudin, and the expression on his face was a perfect example of simultaneous dejection and anger. But he snapped out of it quickly, and Marion thought he might regain the upper hand.

"It's a setup," he muttered. "Duverger wants to get in the game by letting you know that you'll have to go through him if you intend to sell."

"Hold on. So Duverger knows that I'm Magni's daughter?"

"Your father's estate attorney isn't the kind to accept bribes. But Duverger is a very powerful man."

"I knew it. So he may know the specifics of the will too?"

"Most likely. But that's not the problem here. What he's trying to do is slow you down and secure his role as middleman so that you can't try anything without him."

"That's a convoluted plan," Chris intervened. "What makes him think Marion is going to sell? And even if she is, why didn't he just talk to her directly? That would have been way easier!"

"Would Marion have agreed to talk with him if he had taken your direct approach?"

"No more than she would now."

"Ah, but she will now. Because the message was also intended for me. He sent her in search of this figure knowing full well that I would be here. Blackmail—because that's what it's all about—involves two people who know."

"Blackmail?"

"He's aware that any accusation of thievery would tarnish Magni's reputation and possibly make potential buyers suspicious of his collection as a whole."

Marion looked at Chris, and frowned. She was having a difficult time making sense of everything.

Was Gaudin telling the truth? What complex trickery were they all fabricating? She turned to the assistant again when she heard him sigh.

"All right," he said. "I can see that it's time to fill you in. Duverger was the one who introduced your father to the collector I mentioned earlier—Ernsen. Duverger couldn't buy the entire collection on his own, so he asked Magni to go in on it. When Magni laid eyes on the collection, he was mortified. His own collection couldn't hold a candle to those exceptional works of art. Ernsen had breathtaking Olmec pieces purchased in a golden era when objects could be brought out of Mexico. Magni had spent his whole life collecting pre-Columbian artworks, and in his eyes they now amounted to nothing. The next day he purchased the whole lot without telling Duverger. Ernsen made it clear to Ernsen he would never buy another piece from him if he told Duverger. Then Magni fed Duverger a line about Ernsen selling the collection to an anonymous buyer. Duverger didn't learn who it was until the old guy died. He swore to Magni that he'd make him pay one day."

"But Duverger admires Magni."

"Enemies can respect each other, even spend time together. Magni was surrounded by puppets and he pulled the strings. But Duverger was different. He is dangerously clever and, more important, very talented. Your father liked him. He was a worthy opponent. He was pretty much his only competition. And Magni liked their games, even if he thought Duverger was a bit too… How should I put it? Unstable."

"Still, I don't buy your blackmail theory. I'm not Magni, after all. I'm Magni's daughter. We are two entirely different people. I didn't even know my father. Why would he have it in for me?"

Gaudin's tone turned condescending again. "I'm going to tell you something that you need to plant deep in your brain. It's best to use caution when you flirt with the past. You never know what may rise to the surface."

"I still don't understand. Why am I in danger? Why does Duverger care about me? And what's the deal with this sculpture? Who does it belong to—Duverger or Magni?"

"Of all the pieces in Ernsen's collection, it's the only one that eluded your father. It shouldn't be here, and yet..."

"What are you trying to say?"

"By now you know enough to determine the extent of Duverger's power."

"Why are you so secretive? Be clear. How can I defend myself against him if I don't have the information I need?"

Gaudin gave her a cold look.

"You're not going to help me," she said, feeling her anger rise. "That's it, isn't it? You want to stay in control of the collection."

"It's a bit more complicated than that."

"Maybe Duverger will prove to be more talkative than you if I meet with him today and declare my intentions to negotiate a deal." Marion was ready to say anything to get more out of this man.

"You can always try," Gaudin sneered. "But why would he talk if he's not confident that you're in a position to sell? I doubt he'll show his cards as long as you're unable to guarantee anything."

Gaudin kept sending her back to square one. She would have preferred it if he had declared war. She could have assessed what she was up against. But instead, he gave her the impression that he was neither with her nor against her. What if he knew for sure that she didn't pose an imminent threat? That might explain his attitude. He could easily control her moves and protect himself. At any rate, she was becoming convinced that he wasn't scared of her, but rather scared of what she might learn.

This would certainly explain why he was divulging his information with such caution. Maybe he was willing to do anything to preserve Magni's standing in the art world. It was also possible that he feared for himself. Was he scared of Duverger? Apparently Duverger knew Magni's life story by heart. That could make him a dangerous enemy. Or an accomplice…

8

With a heap of discarded clothes at her feet, Marion flirted with her image in the mirror. She had slipped gray silk stockings on her toned legs and wiggled into a form-fitting suit the color of eggplant. She wanted to look businesslike. But she had chosen a blouse with a low neckline that offered a glimpse of her décolletage.

"Just a little bit daring," she said to herself. "It might help."

Yesterday she had decided against going to Alain Ozenberg's gallery. After her meeting with Gaudin, she had only enough strength to stop at the office to check on her calls and e-mails and make an appointment or two. This morning, however, she was taking action. The message was clear: Duverger was capable of putting his money where his mouth was. Poker game or not, Marion would have to deal with him. As for Gaudin, he was still an enigma, more prepared to act defensively than offensively. Or was it the reverse?

Marion stepped back from the mirror and re-evaluated her image. She hadn't felt this sexy in a long time—not since Peter. She dug through her jewelry, clasped a cameo necklace at the back of her neck, and pulled her most expensive pumps out of the closet. Was it overkill? She sat down on her bed.

"Come on, no second-guessing," she told herself and left the apartment.

She got off the metro at the Miromesnil stop and headed south, not noticing the few galleries on Avenue Matignon. She turned left on the Rue du Faubourg Saint-Honoré. Nearing the address, she stopped at a storefront window to readjust her skirt. It was too short. That color on her lips: too dark. And how she'd like a pair of those Christian Louboutin shoes that were staring back at her. What was happening to her?

Reaching Ozenberg's gallery, she took a deep breath, raised her chin, put all doubts out of her mind, and opened the door.

She saw no one inside, just a few cameras pointed toward the sculptures, rendered more humanlike by the honey-colored lighting. The room wasn't big, but the mirrored walls created an illusion of space.

"He's watching me from upstairs," she told herself after spotting a spiral staircase. Marion did her best to focus on a terra-cotta with stumpy arms and legs in the middle of the room. The figure, brandishing a dog-headed stick, looked ready to pounce on the enemy at any moment.

"What do you think?"

She turned around, surprised not by the sound of his voice, which was oddly soft and deep at the same time, but by the question itself. Most art and antiques dealers in this district wore a cloak of arrogance. They bragged about their pieces rather than eliciting comments. Nonchalantly leaning against the staircase railing, Alain Ozenberg was looking at her thoughtfully.

"It seems both petrified and aggressive at the same time. I certainly wouldn't want him for an opponent." Marion had practiced her approach. She intended to present herself as a broker, and this would require choosing her words with care.

"I'm familiar with the effect this figure has on people. I've felt it myself," he said, descending the stairs and walking over to her with a welcoming smile. "Of all the terra-cotta figures I've ever owned, this is one of the most difficult ones to understand. It certainly has a uniqueness, along with a powerful energy." Marion felt his eyes on her.

"You can only imagine what this man went through to carry so much fear into the afterlife," Marion said, still staring at the sculpture.

"Death in those days was often very cruel."

"I admit I'd prefer a peaceful death," she said, surprised by the course the conversation was taking.

"I guess living a well-ordered life is conducive to that kind of end."

"No, I just prefer to confront issues in a civil and rational way."

"Hmm, that sounds like it's coming from someone who's trying to avoid pain at all costs."

She wanted to change the conversation and steer it in a direction that wasn't so personal. But she couldn't resist responding.

"What makes you think we're obligated to endure pain?"

"We're human, aren't we? Pain is inevitable, especially once your soul is on the line."

"I'm more the measured type."

The art dealer fixed his gray eyes on hers. "Something makes me wonder about that."

The silence lingered as they stared at each other. Marion couldn't get a make on him. His questions and opinions were probing, and she should have felt uncomfortable. But she didn't. He was listening to her.

She almost felt like she was back in school, debating a fellow student. This could be fun, she thought.

The telephone rang.

"My business associate. She always checks in about now. Please excuse me."

Marion wanted to focus, but she couldn't. Feeling awkward in her heels, she wandered from one sculpture to the next while stealthily eyeing Ozenberg, who was standing at a writing desk nestled beneath the stairs. His back was turned to her. She figured he was around forty-five. He wasn't especially good-looking. Well, at least not as good-looking as Chris had led her to believe. But he gave the impression of being kind and strong. Poised. Seductive.

"Yes, yes. Wildly attractive."

Ozenberg turned toward her, making eye contact. Marion immediately looked away.

"Calm down," Marion told herself. "He's not talking about you." Or was he?

"She's here… No, no, that hasn't happened to me in a very long time," he said to the caller.

The sound of his voice was making Marion tremble. She was deeply confused—in a way that both puzzled and excited her.

Ozenberg hung up the phone. He didn't move for a moment and seemed lost in thought. Then he slicked his hair back and headed over to her.

"Well, it seems that we've covered quite a bit of ground, but I still haven't asked why you're here."

Marion figured she was looking bewildered, because he took another stab.

"Perhaps you stumbled upon my gallery by accident?"

"No, I came for this sculpture…"

Marion rummaged through her bag and took out a picture.

"You acquired it at an auction. It belonged to Edmond Magni."

"That's correct," he said, examining the image before giving it back to her. "It's an outstanding piece—it has such grace. It's rare to find female figurines from the Gran Pajatén area, but the ones you do find are usually pregnant, like this one. So you're interested in the sculpture?"

"Yes, I'm looking for it."

"Who are you working for?"

"I'm not authorized to tell you."

"In that case, I'm not authorized to sell."

"So it's for sale?"

He grinned. "You're quick on the uptake, aren't you? I'm sorry for giving you the wrong idea. The person who owns that sculpture would never part with it."

"The right proposition could change a person's mind," she answered.

"This object is priceless. At least that's how the owner feels."

"Let me try to persuade him."

"You'll never do that."

"How can you be so sure?"

The businessman walked back to his desk and began going through the messages on his cell phone. Had she gone too far too fast? Had she offended him? She stepped over to him, shifted her weight from one foot to the other as she waited for a response. Her feet, squeezed into the pumps, were throbbing. He finally looked up from his phone.

"Trust me. This client clings to her past. And this sculpture is part of it. Forget about it. You're wasting your time."

She wasn't going to give up. She tried another approach.

"Get that sculpture, and sell it to me," she said in the sweetest voice she could muster.

He laughed. Marion hadn't expected that kind of reaction.

"I like your style," he said at last. "I don't know if I should attribute it to inexperience or excitement. You certainly have a childlike enthusiasm. I love it." He hesitated before whispering, as if speaking to himself, "We'll see how much you really care about this sculpture."

"What do you mean by that?"

"The lady won't quit! Look, you don't have a lot of options here. Either you give up on this, or you turn a blind eye to ethics..." He observed her for a moment. "You probably haven't been in the business long enough to have dealt with this kind of choice. But if you stick with it, you will." He stepped closer. She could feel his breath on her face.

Marion's breathing quickened. Was it because of Ozenberg? Or because she was so close to her goal?

"Forget about what we just discussed. Put it out of your mind. I have another proposition. This one is much more realistic," he said with such natural ease, he didn't seem to doubt her response for a second. "It's a sculpture from the same civilization. It also belonged to Magni. Another masterpiece. An emerald-encrusted warrior."

Marion barely held back a gasp. She quickly looked down at her feet so her eyes wouldn't give her away.

"Don't get too excited," the art dealer let out with friendly sarcasm after a few moments of silence.

"I was thinking," she said, forcing a smile. "Unfortunately, I'm not the only one involved in this decision."

"At least have a look at the piece. Call me tomorrow morning. I'll set up a meeting. And we'll be able to see each other again..."

~ ~ ~

Marion was out of his sight by now. Her feet were barely touching the ground. Chris would never believe she managed to stifle her interest in the warrior while staying unflustered by Ozenberg's charm. It made her almost as giddy as the idea of getting her hands on one of Magni's sculptures.

Marion slowed down and reviewed her final moments with Ozenberg. Something was bothering her. Didier Combes was investigating Chartier's warrior, and another one had popped up at the exact same time. What if it was the same one? She dismissed the thought. Hadn't she told Chris a few hours earlier that thousands of them had been made? The antiques dealer did appear questionable, offering her a not-so-orthodox deal. What had prompted him to do that? Her determination, her excitement, her gullibility? Marion stopped cold in the middle of the sidewalk. What if she were deluding herself? What if the dealer knew nothing about her or the clauses in the will?

Feeling distraught, Marion looked around. She had ended up on a dark and hemmed-in side street. But at the end of the street was the Louvre, enshrouded in a luminous mist.

Marion headed toward the museum. What if she just assumed that everyone was in the know? Wouldn't that make life a whole lot easier?

9

Slouched on a bench in the middle of the Meso-American exhibit, Marion felt like one of those amateur art lovers who eagerly tried to devour the entire Louvre in a single morning. She was now suffering the effects of overdose—a dumbstruck expression on her face and shoeless feet planted in front of her.

She had elbowed her way through the crowds in the lobby under the museum's pyramid—cursing, recalling the "good old days" when there were fewer visitors and I.M. Pei's pyramid entrance had actually made it easier to get in. After taking a ticket from a machine and making it through the turnstile, she had called Chris and told him to meet her there—for moral support. Too late, she realized should have taken the Porte des Lions entrance. Instead, she'd been forced to make her way through the Grande Galerie. When she reached the Spanish collection, she took the stairs down to the Department of Arts of Africa, Asia, Oceania, and the Americas.

She wanted to evaluate the museum's collection and find out if Magni had left his mark, as Bruno had implied. So much for that idea—a huge crowd was packed into this part of the museum, even though it was one o'clock on a weekday afternoon. No doubt it was the novelty factor: some new pieces had been taken out of storage and put on display.

Lulled by the quiet hum of surrounding conversations, Marion started to loosen up and enjoy the streamlined space with its filtered light. But for a few seconds only. As the crowd swarmed around her, the image of the masked swimmers loomed in her head. She straightened up and scanned the museum-goers as they stepped toward each object, backed away, stroked their chins, and tilted their heads. She looked for a face that wasn't focused on the artworks, eyes that lingered on her too long, a hand that slipped suspiciously into a bag or a pocket. Nothing. She shook her head. Would she always be afraid?

She had spent so much of her childhood in this place. Her mother could sit on a bench for hours, focused on a sculpture, a piece of furniture, or a painting. To fight off her boredom, Marion had toyed with each creation in her imagination. Mother-of-pearl marquetry would become a puzzle. She'd transform gemstone inlays into Arabian gardens. Elephant clocks and lion-head mirrors would become fierce jungle creatures. This was how Marion had ended up working with eighteenth-century objects—they had always been a part of her life. But she had only paid attention to multidimensional objects that she could walk around and size up. Two-dimensional paintings left her cold.

Her mother had never cared for primitive artworks. In fact, she hated them.

"At the Citadel de Gran Pajatén, they were great admirers of the moon..."

Marion's ears perked up. She looked for the speaker. Some tourists were gathered around a female tour guide who was addressing them in an animated voice.

"Look at the man's back. It's stooped, as if he were carrying the world. Here, you can see engraved motifs on his ribs. The sun, the moon, stars, planets, the sea, the earth…"

Marion put her pumps back on and walked over to the group. Standing at the back, she looked over the shoulders of the people in front of her to get a glimpse of the piece.

"The nose has two smooth emeralds. This is a major piece, perhaps the most important in the entire pre-Columbian collection at the Louvre."

A few oohs and ahhs came from the crowd, which made Marion even hungrier to see the object. It felt like an eternity before the tribe of art-history lovers moved on to its next stopping point. At last, Marion leaned in toward the crouched figure. None of Magni's sculptures measured up to its beauty. The man's back was rounded like a seashell. His knees were up, and his head was cupped in his hands. His eyes were full of both energy and kindness.

A plaque was affixed to its black velvet base: "Crouched Figure Carrying the World, Gran Pajatén. Donated by Edmond Magni."

The inscription was small and unpretentious.

So here it was: one of the four crossed-off figures on the list she had found in Magni's mansion. What a sneak, she thought. His moves were so perfectly calculated. Making this very special donation to the Louvre had added considerable value to his own collection.

But Marion still couldn't fathom why Magni was so intent on getting rid of those select pieces at the same time and so quickly. And why had he donated one? He stood to make a lot more money by selling them all, and each at a different time. Something else had to be in play. Was Magni planning to chuck it all?

Was Gaudin withholding this tidbit from her? Maybe the personal assistant had even thwarted Magni.

A strange feeling made her look up, and through the glass case she saw two piercing eyes. A diminutive man with a shaved head and an eagle's beak nose was staring. He gave her a friendly smile before turning around and walking away. She followed him with her eyes, troubled by a feeling of déjà-vu. Marion barely felt Chris tugging her sleeve.

"I've been looking for you for ten minutes. It's a madhouse in here." He took her arm. "Come on. Let's go. I don't like being in a crowd this big."

"Wait," she said, pulling away to inspect the other end of the room. But it was too late. The man had already disappeared.

"What is it?"

"Nothing, nothing. Something weird—"

"You feel it too?"

"Feel what?"

"I think someone is following me. I felt it ever since I left the lab. Maybe you've just got me spooked with all your paranoia." His mouth was twitching.

Marion gave him a skeptical look. Should she tell him about the man she just saw?

"This whole situation is beginning to freak me out," Chris said. "It's not just what happened at the pool. It's everything since then too."

"I don't want you to get even more spooked, Chris, but I just saw this man. He was staring at me."

"Is he still here?" The color was draining from Chris's face.

"No, he's gone."

"We definitely need to get out of here. I need a drink."

Marion hesitated and glanced around.

"Let me have a couple of minutes, please. I want to see if any other Magni sculptures are here. Then we'll go. Two minutes, max."

Without giving him time to protest, she elbowed her way from one case to another. She discovered that her father had donated much more to the Louvre. She counted eight pieces from his collection. He appeared to be the only donor, and there were no other pieces from the Gran Pajatén. Nothing from Chorrera, Veracruz, or Huari. Bruno was right. The collection had Magni's stamp all over it.

Marion pointed this out to Chris when she rejoined him. But he wasn't listening. He was scanning the gallery for people who were more interested in him than the artwork.

"Okay, let's get out of here," he said, taking her arm again. "You're going to make me go completely insane."

Once they were safely outside the museum, he stopped and looked at her. "Heels and a suit, huh? Nice. And is that an Ozenberg effect I see sparkling in your eyes?"

As they walked along, Marion gave Chris a full account of her meeting with the art dealer, including his offer to show her the warrior figure. Chris paused as they were about to enter a brasserie, his hand on the door handle.

"What if it's the warrior that Combes is after?"

"I was wondering the same thing. It would be an odd coincidence."

"You're not going to go alone."

"I'm posing as a buyer. I have nothing to fear."

"It could be a trap."

"Well, maybe I wouldn't mind being Ozenberg's victim," she let out, smiling devilishly.

"Marion..."

She inspected the room. It was too bright. Odd for a restaurant that was going for a jungle look, with artificial liana vines all over the place. "Let's find another spot," she said.

"Just one beer. We won't be long."

Chris nudged her toward a table. He pulled out a chair for Marion, took off his coat, and sat down across from her.

"I get it that your meeting with Ozenberg's got you all hyped up—you're a real jumping bean. Still, it's no reason to get reckless."

"Maybe I've just let it take my mind off things," she said. "Don't worry. I haven't forgotten that two thugs tried to drown me." She grinned at him. "So you can stop being a killjoy."

Chris was about to respond when a man and a woman brushed the back of his chair and sat down at the table next to theirs. He glared at the man for a good minute, sending him a message to find another table. He finally gave up and waved over a server.

"A Heineken for me and an espresso for my friend here."

After the server had walked away, Chris leaned toward Marion and whispered, "Something really messed up is going on, Marion."

"Okay, Chris, we're going in circles now. What have you found out? Do you have something new on Chartier?"

"Forget about that guy. He's a waste of time. We'll never get anywhere with him, believe me."

"I'm meeting with Combes tomorrow. There might be progress at his end."

"I doubt it."

"So what's gotten you all worked up then?"

"After talking with you yesterday, I checked the International Council of Museums."

"Why?"

"The ICOM has red lists of archeological objects that are looted and end up on the black market. I also looked up catalogs from official excavation sites that are available to curators and researchers. These are great tools to determine if an artifact is stolen, but it's funny how few people use them. Ignorance is bliss, I guess, and most people don't want to know if something they own has been stolen. Even at our lab, people turn a blind eye."

"Did you find anything on my sculptures?"

"Not a trace. But—"

Chris stopped the waiter before he could pour the beer into his glass. Marion had seen him do this before. Topping off a glass with a perfectly thin layer of foam was a tricky maneuver that he insisted on handling himself.

"Do you know exactly where your dad died?"

"No, not yet. But I was planning on finding out. Everything I've read about him is so vague. Heart attack somewhere in the Andes—I don't know. No reporter bothered to dig into it."

"Find out. It's important."

"Why?"

"Because there's a problem," Chris said after taking a gulp of his beer. "There was a dig in the Piura region—Las Lomas, to be precise. A necropolis. It was the very first one to be tied to the folks at Gran Pajatén. That's crazy, by the way, because you'd think someone would have stumbled across it much earlier. Anyway, it was a gold mine: pumas, human heads, gold shamans with teeth made of pearls and lapis-lazuli, and emerald jewelry. These artifacts were as fine as yours. That's the problem."

Marion observed Chris carefully. She thought she knew what he was about to tell her, but she refused to imagine the worst.

"You understand how things work in Peru. Archeologists depend on tomb raiders. Most of the time, the *huaqueros* get a jump on everyone else. But once they're caught with a big steal, the ground they've riddled with holes becomes the center of attention."

"Is that how the necropolis of Las Lomas was discovered by the rest of the world?"

"Yes. Six royal tombs had already been emptied. Your sculptures were probably part of the looted treasure. It all adds up, Marion: the nature of the pieces, the jewels, the patterns. No way could they have come from anywhere else."

"That's just a theory."

"Marion, even if I'm wrong, and some doubt remains, you have to consider this a possibility. And you know very well why."

She raised an eyebrow. "I could get slammed by the law. Is that it?"

Chris nodded. He turned toward the people next to them. Were they listening in? No worry there. The pair was locked in a heavy make-out session.

"France has ratified the UNESCO Convention, and Peru can ask for restitution," he said in a low voice. "As far as France is concerned, the agreement covers only those works stolen after ratification in the mid-nineties. But that doesn't make much difference, because the UNIDROIT Convention exempts all objects looted from an archaeological site, regardless of when they were taken."

"But think about it, Chris. Peru would have already gone after those sculptures if they came from Las Lomas. What third-world country wouldn't go after the Louvre to get its treasures back? We read about this kind of thing all the time. Renowned museums in Europe and the United States have been forced to return artwork looted from Jewish families during World War II. But when Magni's pieces went to auction, no one batted an eye."

"You still don't get it. When your father sold them, no one but the looters knew about the necropolis. It only made the headlines two years later. By that time the pieces were long gone. Who could say where they came from? But once your sculptures begin to attract media attention—if you put them on the market, for example—Peru might decide to launch an investigation."

"Do you think Peru could demand their return?"

"Yes, given that they're part of a unique and exceptional ensemble. And they're part of a civilization that dominated much of South America for nearly three centuries."

Marion nervously clinked her spoon against the side of her espresso cup. She refused to believe this was true. Prepared to question the most blatant pieces of evidence to make herself feel better, she pursued her defensive strategy.

"But why would Magni have taken even the smallest risk of being found out? He apparently didn't need the money, and nobody was holding a gun to his head and making him turn over any pieces to the Louvre."

"Are you kidding? What risk? Seriously. Your dad was untouchable. He was a major name. He had the freedom to do whatever he wanted."

"They could have questioned him. No one had ever seen Pajatén pieces of that quality before!"

"The industry wasn't going to bother. Magni was counting on that. And besides, he would have protected himself. It's easy to erase the history of an artwork by giving it a fake past. You know the drill. You take it to a small-town auction house without any advertising or catalog and have it sold. You arrange to have it change hands several times and travel from some obscure gallery to an international sale, and that's it. Now you can prove your innocence, just in case."

Chris wasn't drinking his beer anymore. "With you, it might be very different. Face it, Marion, you don't have your father's clout, and you certainly aren't as shady as he was. You're probably going to draw too much attention that you don't want."

Marion swallowed the rest of her espresso. It left a metallic aftertaste. She needed something stronger.

"Can I have a sip of your beer?" she asked, grabbing Chris's glass.

After downing half of it, she leaned back in her chair, closed her eyes, and thought.

"For the sake of argument, let's say you're right," Marion said. "We'll assume, for the moment, that Magni's death has made the Peruvian government sit up and take notice. In order for them to lay claim to my pieces, do they have to know that I'm the one who's in possession of them? As long as I don't show them…"

"You don't have them yet. You'll have to pray none of them end up in auction or are shown somewhere else. In other words—"

"Get them back as soon as possible…" she said softly, wondering if anyone else—Ozenberg, maybe?—was facilitating the task.

Chris paused, then launched in again.

"You're going to say that I'm being cynical, but whatever... Yes, you have to do it quickly. For another reason. The art world is full of vipers who love to spread rumors to make a buck. Even if no investigation is launched, people could start talking. A lot of them would be all too happy to see Magni's reputation destroyed and your collection discredited. It's the perfect way to buy his works on the cheap. Appraisers are always prepared to devalue an object to obtain it more easily. That's for sure."

Marion considered Laurent Duverger's tactics for a moment and dismissed the idea just as quickly.

"This may come as a shock, but I'm not buying your scenario."

Chris threw up his hands and almost spilled his beer. Marion took one of them and smiled.

"I admit you may be right about the tomb raiding. But the rest of it doesn't hold up. You want to know why? You said it yourself: Magni is untouchable. He may be dead, but he's still warm in the grave, and he's still the biggest man in the art world. No one's going after him, because if his reputation's destroyed, everyone else will go down with him. Do you realize the shit storm that would be unleashed if the most important pre-Columbian collection in the world were questioned?"

"The domino theory."

"Well, yeah. It's something that a lot of people with big investments in art would not want to happen. It would be far less costly to eliminate whoever talked too much than to reassess years of acquisitions, confront the scandal, and end up broke. The stakes are too high to let some wild card..."

Chris suddenly gave her a panicked look, and Marion immediately understood. What if she was the wild card? What if the attack in the pool was meant to warn her against making even the slightest attempt to tell the truth? She could be very dangerous if she investigated the issue of her father's stolen goods and misadventures—the looting, the theft. She appeared to have no particular involvement in any underhanded business. Maybe they figured she couldn't be bought. She might even bring the goings-on to light. She had the perfect profile of someone likely to stir up trouble.

10

"Good morning, it's Alain Ozenberg. Sorry to be calling so early. You have a meeting with Helen D at ten thirty this morning at the Ritz-Carlton. Room 207. I hope you'll be able to make it. Otherwise, let me know."

Marion sat up, startled. Was it morning already? The recorded voice was still ringing in her ears. She had forgotten to lower the volume on her machine. She struggled to get out of bed and listen to the message again. No, it wasn't a dream.

"I was supposed to be the one to call him," she muttered as she headed toward the kitchenette to start the coffee. How had he found her? She hadn't given him her card. "Don't freak out," she told herself as she feverishly filled the coffeemaker with water.

This was surrealistic—a meeting with some codenamed woman in a fancy hotel. She picked up her cell phone and entered Chris's number. The call went straight to voice mail.

"Chris, it's me. Call me back ASAP, would you? Really."

Marion kept looking at her phone as she got dressed and gulped down her much-too-strong coffee. She felt sick.

"It's the coffee," she said. "Now, let's go, Chris or no Chris."

~ ~ ~

Marion walked across the octagonal Place Vendôme, a masterpiece of eighteenth-century architecture, her kind of place, one would think. But she found it a little over the top, and she didn't care for the less-than-aesthetically pleasing Vendôme Column right smack in the center.

She pushed open the doors of the Ritz's arched entrance, nearly slamming into the bellboy. The wall clock read ten thirty-five. She was late. Indifferent to the brass, the wall hangings, the shiny mahogany, and the polished leather, she darted toward the nearest stairwell and took the steps two at a time. When she arrived on the second floor, she leaned against the bronze banister to catch her breath and focus her thoughts: here she was, just steps away from her sculpture.

In the hallway, she caught a glimpse of herself in an Italian baroque mirror. Coco Chanel had lived in this hotel for thirty years, and the legendary designer certainly wouldn't have approved of Marion's getup today. She was wearing black Nikes—all that her feet could tolerate after yesterday's adventures—and she had coordinated the rest of her ensemble with the shoes: baggy gray pants and a sky-blue leotard. She looked like a New Yorker ready for a jog in Central Park. Not very professional. Oh well, there was nothing to be done about it now. And someone who was willing to pay millions for art could wear whatever she wanted. Marion smoothed a pesky cowlick and gave herself another application of lipstick. She threw her shoulders back, took a deep breath, and headed down the hall.

Two bodyguards built like sumo wrestlers were manning the entry to room 207. The one squeezed into a blazer with a gun-shaped bulge asked for her ID, while his associate rummaged through her calf-leather bag. What was this about? How ridiculous.

Marion stopped in her tracks when she entered the room. It was practically empty. No furniture, no paintings, no bed. The walls were white. The starkness underscored the beauty of the terra-cotta figure atop a plaster column. There was nothing to detract from it.

Helen D stepped away from one of the windows to greet her. Marion extended a hand without opening her mouth. Her heart was beating too fiercely. The object her father had sent her chasing after, the object that she herself longed to have in her possession—was right there, in the middle of the room. This was the warrior she had been looking for.

Surely the broker was used to seeing prospective buyers grapple with their emotions and ignore common courtesy. She looked unoffended. Without another word, she returned to her place by the window. Her phone was resting on the sill.

The woman was a professional. Of that Marion was certain. She could tell from her stance, even though her hands, with nails painted crimson, trembled just slightly. Why did she keep picking up her phone? Marion approached the sculpture. Was this really the discovery of a lifetime, one that all art collectors dreamed of?

The figure was weeping. Under each almond-shaped eye was a single stream of emeralds. He had a thin and elegant face with a prominent nose, and the right half of his body was covered with geometric designs. He looked noble. It was hard to imagine that this sorrowful Incan was a warrior. And yet, in his right hand he held a deadly looking club.

Marion swallowed hard. She had never experienced anything like this before. The figure seemed alive. Unconsciously she assumed the same pose: head tilted a bit and arms crossed. Her connection with the artifact was so strong, she almost felt merged with it.

"My client is asking three hundred fifty thousand euros."

How long had she been lost in her reverie? Like Sleeping Beauty awakened from her slumber, Marion looked at Helen D as though seeing her for the first time.

Three hundred fifty thousand euros. Should she haggle? She wasn't prepared for that. On what basis, what principles? She wanted this statue. She didn't care about anything else.

"Let me make a call," she said plainly.

Marion pulled her cell phone out of her bag and contacted her bank. She ended the call, dropped the phone back in her bag, and looked at the woman.

"Done."

~ ~ ~

They exchanged no more than four sentences. Marion had never engaged in such a succinct transaction, devoid as it was of all customary niceties. A desire to own that sculpture had engulfed her in a bubble that would have been impossible to penetrate. She had barely even noticed Helen D. If Marion had to describe her right there on the spot, she wouldn't have been able to.

As she walked slowly through the hotel lobby, Marion clutched the beggar's bag holding her treasure. She didn't know what to do with it. Should she stash it at her place?

She glanced at the wall clock above the concierge's head. No time. It was ten past twelve. Didier Combes would be waiting. He was annoyingly punctual. She would have to keep the sculpture with her. Marion took a deep breath and headed toward the Trocodéro Gardens.

11

Spotting Combes alone at a table at the back of the Café de l'Homme, Marion relaxed a bit. From afar, he looked anemic and slightly stooped in this grand dining room, but his welcoming smile was a comfort.

"Marion, how are you? I was afraid you weren't going to make it," he said, wiping his mouth with his napkin and standing up to greet her.

As usual, his gray mustache needed a trim. It was hanging over his upper lip. His silver hair was an inch too long, and his jacket smelled of tobacco.

"I'm so late. I really am sorry."

"I started without you." He waved an arm toward another chair at the table. "Have a seat. We got our usual spot."

Across from her, an expansive window provided a view of the Eiffel Tower, its elegant silhouette overpowered by the massive white-stone Palais de Chaillot.

"Wouldn't you like to take off your coat?"

Marion shook her head. She felt chilled. Her hands, in fact, felt half-frozen. She rubbed them together.

"You look a little pale," he said.

"It's been a rough morning. I just have to snap out of it. I'll be fine," she told him, making sure her bag was still in her lap.

"Can I get you something to drink? A glass of wine?"

"Thanks, but you know me. No alcohol at lunch. Otherwise, I'd have to take a nap. But I am hungry. Starving, in fact. What did you order?"

"Rump steak with tagliatelle. It's the daily special. And it's excellent."

"Okay, rump steak it is. Sounds perfect."

Combes was into his fifties, and his color was sallow from smoking too many Gitanes cigarettes. He wore the same blue or gray-striped suits, regardless of the weather. His slip-on shoes had soles as weathered as a mountain slope. Marion waited for him to start the conversation. They were like two old friends feeling awkward after a prolonged separation.

He played with his fork for a while, and then, without losing his cool demeanor, he started talking. "I need a favor from you, Marion. It's off the record, of course."

"A favor?" she asked, forcing herself to act normal. "Usually I'm the one asking you. How many cases have you solved now? Can anyone come close to matching your record? I wish I had your eye for detail and your photographic memory. You could do my job without spending a minute on the computer."

In fact, Didier Combes was a walking photo library. Art dealers feared him. Some people called him the Man with the Golden Eye—as much because he came from a privileged background as because he could spot an item in a boutique that had been stolen from a residence twenty years earlier. Marion preferred Mr. Nobility because he had the ease of someone with nothing to prove.

"How can I possibly help you?"

"I'd like you to get a lead on this sculpture—maybe Chris mentioned it," he said, handing her a drawing. "It was stolen."

Marion held her breath. She didn't even have to look at it. She knew. She looked anyway.

"Unfortunately, this is all I have. I want to know everything about this sculpture. Where is it from? It's pre-Columbian, but from what region? Was it sold at auction? When? By whom? For how much? It might be recorded in your system. Since cases in this area are rare, we don't automatically get the catalogs. Or some could have slipped by me. Whatever you can find would be helpful."

Marion stared hard at the drawing of the warrior with emerald tears. If only he knew—it was sitting in her lap just inches away from him. Unable to speak, she pretended to take in the details. Finally she looked up at him.

"You should call Bruno. He knows more about this kind of artifact than I do," she managed to say.

"Definitely not. He's not the most discreet guy. No one else should know about this."

"Why not?"

"Eat first," he said, nodding toward the plate that the waiter had just brought over. "Your food will get cold."

She looked at her meal with little interest. The promised tagliatelle weren't the noodles she'd hoped for, but rather multicolored peels of zucchini and carrots. Nouvelle cuisine in a carb-conscious world.

"I'm still listening," she said after a few unenthused bites.

Combes gave her a kind smile, then toyed with the pack of cigarettes on the table.

"The owner, Joseph Chartier, was taken out."

Marion nearly coughed up her meat. She put her fork down and looked at Combes.

"He was murdered. Four days ago, around five in the afternoon. At his place—a duplex in the Marais."

Marion's head was spinning and her heart was leaping out of her chest.

"That sculpture was stolen from him," Combes continued as he pointed to the photo. "The district attorney put me on the case because of the theft. That warrior is our only means of finding the murderer. No information will be revealed about it. You won't hear or see anything on the news until further notice. Not about the murder, not about the theft. They'll just say that Chartier died—not how. Have you heard of him? He wrote *An Apology for Idleness.* Apparently everyone has a thing for him. And the order to find the murderer came from very high up."

Distractedly chewing her meat, Marion tried to size up her situation. "I should just confess," she thought. "I'm taking too big a risk, and it's not worth it. One person has already been murdered. I could be next. I escaped by the skin of my teeth when they tried the first time. I might not be so lucky in the future. I should have come clean when Combes started talking."

She continued to act as though she knew nothing. "Do you have any clues? Or suspects?"

"Are you feeling all right, Marion?" Combes pushed his plate aside. "You're as white as a ghost."

"It's gotten very hot in here, don't you think? And it was freezing just a few minutes ago. Don't worry. I'll be fine."

"Are you sure? They told me at your office that you had been out sick. Was it serious?"

"No, no. It was nothing." She thought her voice sounded more defensive than it should have.

The detective stared at her for a while.

There was no way she'd mention the incident at the pool. That would just bring on a slew of unwanted questions. She hadn't told anyone at work the real reason she had taken time off, and she didn't think Combes would know—unless he had found out that she was in the hospital. It was possible that he had made some progress in his investigation and was now aware that she was the daughter of the infamous Edmond Magni. But considering their friendship, he would have been more direct. Nonetheless, she wasn't taking his cunning nature for granted.

"So have you made any progress?"

"No, nothing. I met with a few experts to find out if the sculpture had passed through their hands. I hit brick walls. It seems as if the little masterpiece has no history."

"You didn't find a sales receipt at Chartier's place?" she asked, surprised to have regained her composure so quickly. She had never been a good liar.

"Nothing. No sales receipt. No certificate of authenticity. I'm sure everything related to this sculpture was stolen along with the figure itself. Chartier was diligent about his paperwork. There's not a chair or a rug at his place that doesn't have a detailed record and accompanying picture. But as far as this sculpture's concerned, some X-rays and an analysis from an authentication lab were all that we could dig up. And no luck when we asked to see the file—they couldn't find it. It's been like that from the start. We're not getting anywhere. Nothing but dead ends."

"Did you look into an insurance policy?"

"No insurance. Insuring these things can cost too much, and you need impeccable documentation."

Combes grabbed the salt shaker and rolled it between his hands. Marion focused on his nicotine-stained fingers.

"My wife wants me to quit smoking. It's a sign of love, I suppose."

Marion forced a smile. But it wasn't Combes's cigarette habit that she had on her mind. She was thinking about her trip to the Ritz. Thank God no one knew. She went back over her meeting with Ozenberg. The figure had become available for purchase as soon as it was stolen. She couldn't picture the art dealer as a murderer. Why had he taken such a risk with her? Marion could easily report him to the police. What made him think she'd retreat into silence?

"Are you having coffee or dessert?"

"I'd love some coffee."

Didier Combes gave her another smile. She wasn't fooled, though. She knew in her bones that not a single detail got by him—a movement in the room, a facial expression, a squirm, a gesture. He mentally recorded everything.

"Nothing else was stolen?" she asked to break the silence.

"Nope, and that's another mystery. He had enough at his place to feed every antique shop on the planet. Masterpieces galore. This made it very hard for the maid. It took her a whole day to figure out what was stolen. We're lucky we have the drawing. Chartier let her dust the piece, but she hadn't committed all the details to memory." The detective let out a phlegmy cough. "I think we finally wound up with a good-enough composite. The sculpture won't be confused with another piece."

"The decaf?"

The waiter's voice was so soft, Marion couldn't tell whether he was asking them or the people at the next table.

"That's for me." Didier Combes pushed aside his half-full glass of red wine. He dropped three cubes of sugar into his coffee and stirred it slowly.

"Where was I?"

"Nothing else was stolen."

"Ah, yes. Anyway, it's a total disaster. We don't have any fingerprints, either. Our guy covered his tracks."

Combes stopped talking. Marion wondered if he was expecting her to jump in.

"It wasn't a break-in?"

"Chartier answered his intercom. The man—or woman, I'm not making any assumptions—was expected. He had prepared a tea tray."

Ozenberg, Chartier… Marion knew the two men could easily have crossed paths.

"Was there anything in his datebook? Any mention of friends or family?"

Combes shook his head. "I'm really counting on you to shed some light on this."

Marion found his tone peremptory. Did he, in fact, know more than he was letting on? She took a good look at his face, but it wasn't revealing any ulterior motives.

"I'll do my best," she said in a voice that she hoped sounded detached. "But you know how our computers work. Without a photo, don't expect any miracles. And I'm really not the best person to handle this. Bruno would be a much bigger help. He's got a lot of connections."

"That's exactly why I don't want you saying anything to him. He's too much of a gossip."

"And you think we'll be able to find it without any extra backup?"

"We might not need it. This was no ordinary theft. This may have been a special request. A collector perhaps. Or an act of revenge. If either is the case, the ordinary channels may be of no use."

A heavy silence sank in. The detective stared at her without blinking. Finally he spoke. "I wonder what's so important about that damned warrior that people would kill for it."

~ ~ ~

Her head pressed against the window, Marion slumped into the seat of the taxi that was taking her to SearchArt. She was relieved to be alone. Combes had been concerned and had offered to drive her to the office, but she had refused. He didn't insist.

She wanted to clear her mind, but a thousand questions were tormenting her. How could Ozenberg act so fast? Art amateur—yeah right! What a fake. She had to face facts. While some people were trying to scare her into giving up, others—she didn't know who—seemed to have a lot to gain from helping her. Enough to commit murder? There was a likely pot of gold at the end of this rainbow if she sold the collection. It would be a bonanza for dealers. But Ozenberg a killer? She didn't buy it. His scandalous reputation didn't make him a murderer.

And what about her? She had crucial evidence. She could be charged with possession of stolen property, perhaps even implicated in a murder. And why? For wanting something so badly she'd do anything for it? She had become another person overnight, and it had happened so naturally. She had thought of herself as conscientious, always wanting to do the right thing. But now she felt no remorse. And after spending what seemed like a lifetime constructing a protective wall around herself, she had barged across a moral barrier without giving it a second thought. Yes, she was a nervous wreck, but who wouldn't be in the same situation?

"Seriously, do you still want me to go along the Seine?"

The driver turned around and looked at Marion. She sat up and glanced at the traffic. It was bumper-to-bumper.

"Go whichever way you want, but definitely not along the Seine," she instructed, suddenly fixated on the steering wheel. A copy of the Torah was fastened to it with the help of two thick rubber bands. There was something comical about the way the book tilted left or right, depending on where the taxi was heading.

"How can you read and drive at the same time?"

"Only at red lights," the man replied.

"Turn around. I changed my mind. Take me to 64 Rue du Faubourg Saint-Honoré."

12

Didier Combes followed Marion's taxi with his eyes for several minutes, until he heard someone calling his name. Combes grumbled and turned toward the voice. René Joseph, homicide's star player was yelling from the window of his Peugeot.

"You're such a curmudgeon, Combes. At least say hello."

"If you're planning to look over my shoulder every minute of this investigation, it won't be long before I have a big bang-size headache," Combes said. He was a lone wolf. He worked his cases by himself and as he saw fit. But his unit tracked stolen artworks, not murderers, so the brass had paired him with Joseph on this one.

"Will she be able to help?" Joseph asked.

"Hard to say. She looked worried—and tired. Apparently she was sick. I thought she was going to faint right at our table. I didn't tell her about the mutilations. They made me gag with all my years on the force."

Combes couldn't get the images of the man's body out of his head: the thumb of the right hand crudely chopped off, with only a purplish and puffy stump remaining. Both eyes removed with surgical precision. And under each bloody socket, a row of little circles cut with a scalpel.

This bat-shit murderer had also practiced his artistry on Chartier's torso. Once again using a scalpel, he had covered the entire right side with geometric figures. A compass couldn't have achieved better results. The incisions were perfect. The culprit was exacting, diligent, and smart. He had dabbed vinegar on the wounds to staunch the bleeding. And when he was done with his work, he had thoroughly scrubbed the bathroom tiles. They were pristine and shiny against the maimed body.

"Yeah, he left a real piece of art," Joseph said, laughing at his own joke.

Combes looked at the man. He wasn't the kind of guy who'd be comfortable in an art gallery, but he had a sixth sense when it came to police work.

"I should have told her. I'm sure they had something to do with the sculpture. I was thinking about what you said when we examined the body: 'Our eyes and hands—our biological identity.'"

In fact, he had fixated on this thought. "In the past two days, I've read a lot on the symbolism of body markings and engravings. It seems that in many civilizations, camouflage, tattoos, scarring, and mutilation are signs of your membership in a group. You could prove your bravery by undergoing symbolic scarring. In the Americas and in Africa, the human body was considered a kind of artistic medium. Disfiguring the head or ears and painting or scarring your body enhanced your beauty. You'd become living art."

"Only this time, it's dead art," Joseph said, and then thought for a minute. "Funny isn't it. It seems that everyone has tattoos and piercing these days. Body art. What goes around, comes around."

"Yeah, well, Chartier didn't volunteer for his body engravings. In fact, he was dead when the artist began wielding his scalpel. So what was the killer's intent? Did he want to make Chartier his life-size sculpture, create an ideal body, distinguish him from a community of like-minded people, or, rather, initiate him into it?"

"That's where the girl could help."

"I'll call her later. Anyway, I'm heading back to the office."

"Want a ride?"

"No, I'll walk," he said, reaching into his pocket and taking out a navy blue wool cap. With it came a magnifying glass.

"You've got to be kidding," Joseph said. "I was told you were old school, but that's last century. What else have you got in your pockets?"

"You really want to know?"

Combes pulled out the items one by one: a knife, a toothbrush, a disposable razor, a needle, thread, two packs of cigarettes, a lighter, and four books of matches. "When I started in this job, we used to actually travel—I would hop on a train or plane to Brussels, Milan, or Geneva at a moment's notice. Nowadays, you guys just search the Internet, but I'm always ready to go. You never know."

Grinning, René Joseph whipped out his smart phone and took a picture of Combes stuffing his paraphernalia back in his pockets.

"There you go, sending more data out into the technological universe. Whatever happened to paper and pens? I'm wondering if you'll even know how to turn the pages of a book ten years from now. You're just like the kids in my department, always running to their databases. They don't trust their memories anymore. You're becoming mechanized men."

"That said, I hear you're the best they've got, as old-fashioned as you are."

"My time may have come and gone. The days of visiting auction houses and schmoozing with art dealers are numbered. Now you can pull up high-definition images of artworks in minutes without even leaving the office. It's not the way I work. I have to admit that I've been giving more thought to leaving the force. But don't get your hopes up. We've got a particularly gruesome murder to solve."

"And if you just stand there, you're going to catch a cold, old man. So get in or get going."

"Catch you later."

~ ~ ~

Combes walked along the river at a steady clip, his collar up and his head down to shield himself from the bitter wind. He was thinking about Marion. She definitely wasn't the same Marion he usually met for lunch. She was deathly pale, practically translucent. But she seemed more feminine too, sexier… It was actually crazy how much she reminded him of Josephia, a Georgian woman he had fallen in love with while on a mission to retrieve a stolen icon in Tbilisi. Her thin face, gray and stormy eyes, and proud bearing… He had never made the connection before.

But seriously, he had never seen Marion so distracted. She was usually in a good mood, poised and happy to see him. Kind of like a kid, actually. Of course, he was no fool. She flattered his ego by giving him the impression that she was his student. It was her way of getting him to confide.

Maybe she really was sick.

Why hadn't he told her about the lacerations on Chartier's body? Ritual slayings were so out of his league.

"I should have," he muttered as he moved along the river.

The detective stopped in front of the metro station by the Alma Bridge. He weighed taking the subway back to the office. He'd get there faster. But what was the rush? The computers weren't going to help him. No, he needed to do this his way. He needed to talk to someone on the inside. And he knew just the man to see: his pal Pierre, a stylish gentleman who was always in the know.

Pierre Roux had known early on that he wanted his life to be all about works of art, particularly the pursuit of them. He had gotten his start at the age of sixteen at the Drouot auction house. He was one of Drouot's *commissionnaires*, an elite group composed primarily of men from Savoie and Haute-Savoie. Easily identifiable because of the black suits they wore, the *commissionnaires* transported items to the Drouot site, set them up, presented them for sale, and then took them to the buyers' homes. This is how Pierre had developed relationships with all the merchants, auctioneers, and collectors. Now he was an antique dealer. If there was something to be known, he would know it.

Combes looked at his watch. Perfect. Roux would be finishing off his lunch.

The first words out of his friend's mouth were as good as a mirror: "Didier! What a surprise, but all I need is another wet blanket. Don't tell me you're coming here with a pile of your own problems, or I'll have to send you back to that bleak police station of yours."

"Do I look that bad?" Combes said, smiling.

"That's better," Roux said, opening his arms to his friend. "You should smile more. Makes you look younger. He playfully pinched the detective's cheeks. "Am I happy to see you. Let me get a look at you. It's been forever. Come on, we'll start cocktail hour a little early." He closed the door. "I could use a break from my problems right now."

Didier Combes had forgotten just how portly the secondhand art dealer was. He marveled at the man's ability to make his way through his space, as big as he was and as stuffed as it was. Combes glanced around the room and saw oriental screens, a Louis XIII stool, a baroque statue of Jesus, ship replicas, an Arman sculpture, a Vladimir Velickovic painting, ciboriums, china, crystal, and piles of old books. Roux had eclectic tastes. Roux liked all beautiful works, regardless of when they were made. His finances rarely allowed him to keep the objects long before selling them. But in a way, they all stayed with him, because he remembered every detail, every curve, every anecdote.

"Look at these," the dealer said, pointing to a pair of Louis XV chairs in the corner. Someone had brutally slashed the upholstery. "I've just brought them home. They're battered, but they're not ready for the cemetery yet. I'll disassemble them. Who knows? A little old man may have stashed a wad of bills inside one. Not everyone trusts the banks."

At the back of the room, lit by a beautiful Murano glass chandelier, a small Louis XVI rolltop bureau served as a worktable. On it lay a magnifying glass, gold dust, sanding paper, pieces of glass, semiprecious stones, and clock movements. Roux brushed aside his tools to make room for two wine glasses and a bottle of white, one of his many indulgences. The fifties-era fridge stuck out like a sore thumb in this room full of classy collectibles, but the dealer needed a place to keep his wine chilled.

"Let's get down to business," Roux joked. "We're gonna destroy this guy. It's a wonderful wine—a 2005 Saint-Péray that I came across in Tain l'Hermitage."

"Sounds good. So tell me about all these problems of yours," Combes said after Roux had settled into his bergère armchair.

"My father passed away last month. It's complicated, not easy for me to talk about," The antiques dealer plunged his nose into his glass, took a noisy gulp, and continued. "When you lose a parent, you start thinking about your own mortality. I'm sixty years old, and it hit me that I have more years behind me than in front. I confess I've been dwelling on this." Roux gave his friend a faint smile. "You could say I'm depressed. Yep, me. Depressed. And Nicole's no help. She keeps nagging me to get out of my funk and change my lifestyle. You know: lose weight, quit drinking. Like it's all that easy. Thirty-five years of living together and not an ounce of sympathy! Can you believe it?"

Didier Combes sipped his wine without saying anything for a while.

"What about the shop? You're not planning to give it up, are you?"

"I don't know. I don't seem to have the passion for it these days. For the first time in my life, I don't know what I want to do. I should be scared, but oddly, I'm not. I just don't care. The EEG is flat."

What a strange day this had become. First Marion, now Pierre Roux. He had always been so driven, so confident, with a set of sophisticated interpersonal skills developed in his twenty years as a *commissionaire.*

"Anyway, enough about me," Roux said. "What's up with you, old pal? You're not visiting on a whim, are you?"

"I haven't seen you in quite a while, and I always value our visits, my friend," Combes said. "But I'm also here for a reason. I'm investigating the theft of a pre-Columbian sculpture."

"Stolen from Chartier?"

Combes raised an eyebrow. He knew Pierre Roux was well connected and an expert in gathering information, but this case was highly confidential. And Roux was clearly pleased with himself. Combes did his best to look impassive, handing the dealer his empty glass.

"Could I have a refill? I'm a fan."

"I'm glad you like it. It may be a bit too chilled. It has—"

Combes cut him off. "Just let me drink the wine, won't you? So, did you know Chartier?"

"Just by name. I would have loved bargaining with him. The guy was a real art aficionado. But he only rubbed elbows with the most elite decorators and the dealers who owned the fanciest mansions. He was the kind of guy who bragged about where an object came from and who it belonged to. He hardly ever relied on his own judgment. And yet he didn't miss a thing. Did you check out the stash at his place? I heard it was full of masterpieces. Is that true?"

"Yes, there are some very lovely pieces in his home," Combes replied. "What about the stolen sculpture?"

Pierre Roux adjusted his red-and-black silk tie, which always accessorized his black suit. Even though he had long ago given up his job as a *commissionaire*, he had never changed the way he dressed. Combes wondered if Roux wanted to remind people of his humble beginnings.

"I don't know what it looks like. Just that it loosens lips." Roux seemed less depressed now. In fact, he had a mischievous look on his face, as though he were thrilled to be playing the role of informant.

"It's like royal families. Everyone thinks they know what's going on, but really nobody knows a thing. Everyone has a theory about that sculpture," Roux continued. "Some people swear it's a fake. Others claim it was bought from Magni. You know who I'm talking about—the pope of pre-Columbian art who died not too long ago. There've actually been a lot of deaths recently. All big names in the art world too."

Combes tapped a cigarette on the worktable to pack the tobacco. There was no hiding his irritation. He was mad at himself for failing to find even the smallest lead. Had he really lost his touch? He was annoyed with Roux, too, for being so much in the know. He understood that the dealer was a fount of information, but he had underestimated the extent of the man's relationships. One thing was certain: they had to do a better job of keeping the investigation under wraps. Leaks were unacceptable.

"A fake. To kill for a fake... That seems so ridiculous to me," Roux continued. "But anyhow, what I've told you is strictly gossip, and the part about Magni doesn't make sense either. He never sold anything to anyone."

Despite his weight, Pierre Roux stood up with tigerlike agility, as if he had just spotted someone stealing one of his artworks. "I'm just talking bullshit," he said, heading toward an area of the shop where books lined the wall.

Combes sipped his wine and allowed the dealer to continue talking. Roux pulled a book off a shelf and started walking back to him.

"Here we go. Take a look at this catalog. It's a collector's item." Roux held it out to Combes but didn't let go. "There are less than two hundred of these—a very limited edition with a crocodile-skin cover. Rare and expensive. A little museum in itself. It's from an extraordinary pre-Columbian art auction. For security reasons—allegedly—you were let in only if you had an official invitation. I think there was even a president in attendance—from either Guatemala or Venezuela. I can't remember exactly."

The dealer pulled his chair closer to Combes and sat down.

"This auction caused one hell of a ruckus."

"Not around our office, apparently." Combes blurted this out more vehemently than he intended.

"You'll have to clue in your higher-ups at the cop shop. They need to let you guys out more."

Pierre Roux flipped through the catalog, finally pointing to a picture.

"Magni," he said, leaning back in his chair. "Heavy stuff, right?"

His eyes glued to the page in question, Didier Combes was speechless. He had poured over dozens of auction catalogs, and now, by pure chance, he had stumbled upon the warrior. This picture didn't exactly match the composite, whose features weren't as sharp, but this was definitely the sculpture.

There was something else the composite hadn't shown, and now it was as clear as day. The lesions on Chartier's body were identical to the markings on the warrior. The small circles carved under Chartier's eye sockets matched up with the emerald teardrops beneath he warrior's. The same geometric designs were on Chartier's body. And the mutilated thumb. Chartier had been stripped, shaved, and done up, all for the purpose of serving as a human replica.

"So is that it?" Pierre Roux asked.

Combes ignored the question. He leafed through the pages, trying his best to look calm. "Let me ask you something. Is Duverger the best appraiser when it comes to this era?"

Two similar sculptures were displayed majestically against a dark and shiny backdrop. They also had emeralds, and the same owner was listed. Combes finally had something to go on. Something big.

Roux gave him a knowing look before responding. "Yes, he's the go-to guy. But good luck trying to squeeze any information out of him. The man is very tight-lipped. The only way he'll talk is if it serves his own interests."

Combes had already approached Duverger and hadn't met with any success. According to his informant, the appraiser had only a rough drawing of the warrior and had never seen Chartier's collection. Combes felt lighter now. He'd jump back into the fray tomorrow. With photos.

"Who are the other heavyweights in this market?"

"Ruiz, Dallon, Jaine... Ozenberg too... Yeah, Ozenberg, even though he's not as recognized as the others. I think that's about it for the antiques dealers. But I'm sure I'm not telling you anything you don't already know."

Indeed, they were all on the detective's list, but he hadn't gotten anywhere with any of them either.

"Can I borrow this?" he asked, closing the catalog.

Roux hesitated.

"Wouldn't you rather make copies? My scanner's right over there. It makes very good prints."

"Could I buy it from you then?"

"This catalog's not for sale."

"Can't you help me out here?" Didier Combes gave Roux an earnest look. He knew his friend wasn't going to part easily with the catalog. Like everything else crammed inside his shop, it was a treasure. Pierre Roux would have to be charmed and convinced that Combes simply had to have the catalog. That was his way. Roux needed to start a back-and-forth, create a bond, build excitement, and finally strike a deal. It didn't matter if it was with an acquaintance or an old friend.

"I'm almost certain that the sculpture in this catalog is a match with what I'm looking for. But I need to make sure, and to do that, I need the catalog."

"You promise to bring it back? And quickly? I want to know how this all turns out."

"No information leaves this shop. And please try to find out more about Magni. It won't be our software programs that'll tell us about his past. I want to know everything about the man, his collection, his heirs…"

"You mean his heir. Singular. That's only recently been discovered. Even she probably doesn't know yet that she's entitled to an empire. Her name's Marion Spiler or Spicer. Something like that. Yeah, Spicer. That's it."

13

She really *really* wanted to ask him. At least, she thought she did.

She was heading back to his shop with the intention of asking him point blank. In what way and how deeply was he involved? Ozenberg had to answer. He'd clear everything up. Or would he? She took a few deep breaths. In any case, she had to see him. And the idea made her tingle.

The shop was empty. She figured he was upstairs, watching her, the same as the last time. Her heart was racing. She climbed the stairs slowly, gripping the cold railing. She reached the top and found the entrance to a darkened room. She inched forward, alert to the softest sound, the slightest movement. That was when she inhaled his musky cologne. He was right there, in front of her, leaning against the wall. Towering, silent, wearing a black suit, his disheveled silvery hair framing a composed face with a powerful nose. He was challenging her with his gray eyes. Was it the adrenaline, his raw sexual gaze, his intoxicating smell? He wanted her. He'd have her. She knew it. He felt it.

He stepped aside to let her pass. Their bodies brushed. For some reason, she headed toward a small empire desk glowing in the light from a window. He followed her with his eyes. She felt provocative, open, compliant even. She put her bag on a chair to keep it within sight and slowly walked around the desk while grazing the base of the lamp on it with her fingers. The man didn't move. He simply watched. She started moving around the room.

Everything was worthy of attention, and yet nothing kept it. Her hand paused on the pedestal of a sculpture, a telephone, the armrest of a couch. But spellbound, she was drawn back to him.

Just as she was about to glide past him, Ozenberg reached out and pinned her against the wall. Her breathing stopped instantly, her lips inches from his. He slid his hand down her back and into her waistband. He slipped it into her panties and pulled her bottom toward his groin. She was burning and shaking at the same time. Then, with a powerful but careful move that took her by surprise, he brought her gently to the floor. He kissed her face, gently, under each eye, making his way to her neck. He unbuttoned her blouse, and took her breasts in his hands. He teased her nipples with his supple fingers. A second later, they were desperately ripping off their clothes. Their bodies were one.

Her hips were arched in excitement. She longed for him to thrust himself into her, but it was his tongue that started exploring her every secret. He spread her with his fingers and slowly licked, from bottom to top and down again. He put two fingers inside her and stroked her there, firmly and evenly.

How did this man know exactly how to please her? It was uncanny—almost scary. For a second Marion considered stopping rather than surrendering. But that was when he forced her legs higher and plunged into her. He moved deeper and deeper, faster and faster, sweating, panting, burying himself. At the moment of ecstasy he pulled out and ejaculated on her stomach.

She moaned with pleasure and pain, having expelled all her loneliness. With her legs still spread, she held onto him until he rolled to his side and caught his breath. He looked at her long and hard. "That was beautiful," he finally said. "You're beautiful."

She felt spent as she nestled next to him. They were quiet for a long time. He held her in the crook of one arm, and with his free hand, he caressed her body, his fingers forming spirals and shapes, sometimes gently, sometimes forcefully.

"Beautiful. Like artwork," he kept saying.

She enjoyed the playfulness. It calmed her.

After what seemed like both hours and minutes, she asked him what she needed to know.

"Did you have anything to do with Chartier's murder?"

Ozenberg pulled away and sat up. His features looked heavier. His jaw was twitching.

"Marion, who told you he was murdered?"

"The cop who's leading the investigation."

"The police have already gotten to you?"

Marion stared at him. She didn't know what to think or do. Tell him more to calm him down? Keep quiet? Wait until he opened up to her? He was apparently more involved than he wanted to admit.

She sat up too and broke the silence. "We work together. He's looking for information about that sculpture. He doesn't have any leads."

Ozenberg looked at her even more intensely. Was he trying to figure out if she was telling the truth? It was making her uncomfortable, like a child caught for doing something bad.

"You haven't answered my question, Mr. Ozenberg," she said defensively. "Were you behind the murder?"

How crazy was that? The two of them had just made love, and she couldn't call him by his first name.

"Do you think I was?"

"No."

"Then I wasn't."

"Don't play games with me!" she cried out, turning away to avoid his eyes.

"What makes you think I'm playing games?" he threw out with such vehemence, there was no room for objection.

"You had to know the sculpture belonged to Chartier."

"I knew the sculpture was on the market, and for the record, I wanted it. But I wasn't the only one. It was sold to a higher bidder. So that's that."

"And what if I hadn't bought it?"

He was giving her a snide look.

"You knew about the will," she seethed. "Of course you knew. You took a pretty big risk. I could have ratted you out. You didn't seem too eager to help me the first time we met. That *Woman with Child* sculpture I was looking for..."

"I was testing you. That said, I still don't know how to help you get that figure."

Ozenberg rose to his feet, pulled on his pants, and buttoned his white monogrammed shirt. He headed toward the back of the room to open his minibar. Marion got up too and started dressing.

"Here, this'll be good for you," he said, handing her a glass of whiskey. "Have a seat." He took her by the arm, guided her to the couch, and sat down close to her.

"Do a lot of you know the provisions of my will?"

"Marion, Marion..." he said as he fixed a strand of hair that had fallen over her forehead. "You have such striking eyes."

"Alain, this is serious."

"Since Magni died, the art world's been buzzing. His collection—it's like a godsend for everyone. I don't know if you realize how—"

"People will kill for it, yeah," she answered, once again keeping her distance. "So I'm in danger then?"

He didn't answer.

"Your silence isn't very reassuring."

"It's not a very reassuring situation."

"And these networks, these people who steal for you and other people. You know who they are. We could follow their trail."

"It's a blurry trail, Marion. You saw Helen D. She's a fourth intermediary—at least. And they change all the time."

"But they get paid. We could follow the money trail."

"There are handlers and one-purpose companies used for a single transaction. Then they disappear. They're created to collect money and send it somewhere else, like an offshore account, which sends it somewhere else again. By the time an investigation gets under way, the money has already been dispersed to hundreds of similar accounts. It can't be traced. Are you sure you want to talk about this right now?" He had started to stroke her breasts. "Maybe there are other things we could be doing."

She shivered, not knowing whether it was the fear or his presence that was giving her the goose bumps. His melodious voice, his breath, his scent... She pressed herself against him and put her head on his shoulder.

"There'll never be a good time. I just want to get this figured out as soon as I can."

"We have all the time in the world to talk about it."

"I need to know."

"Do you always get what you want?"

"Tell me more…"

He breathed in the smell of her hair.

"You're stubborn, but I like it," he said, pulling her onto his lap.

14

He had never felt this outraged, this crushed. Chartier's warrior had gotten away. He had just discovered this after hours making more phone calls than he could count in search of the incompetent intermediary he'd chosen. The man was a slippery eel.

Duverger had a bitter taste in his mouth, one that he swore he would never taste again. The appraiser was a sore loser, so he made sure he never lost. He much preferred countering to being countered. Born to a family of diplomats and the youngest of five "good-for-nothing brats"—as they were called—he had too often been rejected and pushed to the side-lines while his older siblings took the trophies. That was long ago. Now his own trophy had slipped from his grasp, and he had no intention of just waiting for it to resurface.

He pulled his cigarette case from his leather jacket. It was empty. He threw it against the car seat and tapped the chauffeur on the shoulder with so much anger, the driver almost swerved off the road.

"A Cuban, Marco. In the glove box. There's got to be a few left."

"No one does that to me," he muttered, sinking deeper into the luxury car's cream-colored leather seat.

Everything should have gone down perfectly. The members of his ring had acted as soon as Chartier's sculpture hit the market. They had neutralized all other middlemen and had appointed a single acquirer. With the competition significantly weakened, they were set to acquire the piece at a price that was significantly lower than its value. Then they would organize an unofficial auction and sell the sculpture at a price much closer to its real value. The members of the ring would split the profit: the difference between what they had paid for the sculpture and the price that it fetched at the second auction. Although it was illegal, such collusion was common. Duverger's intermediary was supposed to be the bidder who acquired the sculpture. But Ozenberg had derailed the whole plan. He had swooped in and made off with the piece himself.

Laurent Duverger nervously tapped his foot.

Ozenberg—a man with a lopsided life, a man who was obsessed with money and pleasure—had won by a nose. And at the last second! How had he beat out the best in the business? How did he have the moxie or the money to short-circuit the collusion? How had he worked the game so cleverly that the sculpture had wound up in Marion's hands?

"I should've handled this personally, but it was too risky," he said to himself. "No one can know I'm in the same arena as Marion. What a mess."

Inside his Bentley-turned-private-club with its big-screen entertainment system and minibar, Laurent Duverger opened his fridge and poured himself a glass of Russian vodka. He downed it in one gulp. Then he took a deep breath. His facial muscles released their tension as the alcohol took effect. The appraiser needed to start plotting again.

"I must have that warrior. I don't care what it takes. I must have it," he said out loud.

15

SearchArt was dead quiet. Sophie, who usually sat behind the reception desk, was nowhere to be seen. Good, Marion thought. There was nobody around to sense her inner turmoil. All she could think about was Alain Ozenberg.

This was weird, though. Sophie was always at her desk. It was late in the morning but too early for lunch.

Marion opened her office door. Then Bruno's. Nobody home. Just when she was about to inspect the last office she heard someone racing down the stairs from La Medici's office. She turned around.

"Sophie?"

"Good. You're here. I was all by myself. You know how much La Medici hates it when no one else is in the office." Sophie took on a bossy tone whenever their fearless leader was away.

"Where is she?"

"She left yesterday for the New York Antique Fair. You forgot she was going, didn't you?" Sophie glared at Marion. Was she supposed to feel guilty? "La Medici's already called for an update on the Duverger case."

Even when she was on the other side of the ocean, the hounding never stopped.

"What about Bruno?" Marion asked. "I thought he'd be here."

"He's at the doctor's office. He left work with a stomach thing, but he didn't look sick to me. I don't know what's gotten into everyone. You're all off in a hundred different directions."

"Do I have any messages?" Marion was tired of Sophie's complaints.

"Detective Combes called, and Bruno has a file he wants you to see."

Marion started toward Bruno's office. "Okay, Marion, focus," she muttered once she had closed the door behind her. It was time to put aside thoughts of Ozenberg—along with his voice, his moves, and their innovative lovemaking positions. She stared at Bruno's collection of art books, all perfectly aligned. Not a single spine hung over the edge of the shelves. Bruno had probably hidden the file in an old book about the Museo del Oro. This was how they passed documents to each other whenever one of them was out. The boss methodically checked computers, drawers, and trashcans for messages. Marion had asked Bruno to compile every article on Magni that he could find. She wanted to know exactly where and how the man had died.

Indeed, a small catalog envelope was tucked between the pages of the book. And inscribed neatly in big black letters on the front was her father's name. Bruno's OCD came across in the smallest of details.

"Couldn't find the auction catalog," Bruno had written in a note. "Go straight to the source. Call Mr. Rambert, and tell him we're colleagues. I've got more news for you. Will tell you in person."

Mr. Rambert, how about that.

Marion sat down and tried to calm herself. Under different circumstances, she'd have paced in front of the phone before making a call aimed at prying out the names of the sculptures' owners. But the fact that the auctioneer had pounced on her like a vulture made her feel more daring. Then again, she thought, it could be the Ozenberg Effect.

She entered the number and asked for Mr. Rambert. His secretary, who had most likely heard him spew her name dozens of times, put her through immediately.

"Our conversation was a bit brief the other day. I wasn't able to call you back until now," she said, paying phone etiquette no mind.

"I understand. How may I help you?"

"I need you to clear something up for me."

"I'm all ears."

"I recently learned that you handled three sculptures belonging to Edmond Magni at an auction a few years ago. Those were the only ones he ever sold. Do you know why?"

"Oh, there was nothing surprising about that," Mr. Rambert responded without hesitation. "Your father said he was bored and wanted a fresh start. That happens to collectors like him all the time. When they've been at the top of their game for a while, they start looking for new conquests."

So that was it? He wanted a clean slate? The answer didn't satisfy Marion. "Why just three sculptures? Why not ten or a hundred?"

"We had to build hype for his first auction. Everyone was ready to jump in. He had us show only the most extraordinary pieces in order to surprise the market and keep them in suspense until the next sale. Those were the most breathtaking auctions anyone had ever seen. We agreed to organize the next ones as quickly as possible to keep up the momentum."

"So what happened next?"

"Your father was taking his time to make the arrangements, and then, unfortunately—"

"Did you know which pieces he was planning to sell next?" she asked quickly, afraid the man would clam up.

"Do you intend to sell the collection?"

The hunger in the auctioneer's voice was palpable. He'd been an easy victim to bait.

"Yes, part of it. But not before putting together a solid catalog…"

"We can help with that."

"I know. That's also why I called. I need to know who owns the sold-off pieces so I can provide a detailed description of them—assuming the owners agree to be mentioned."

"Two of them probably won't have a problem with being mentioned. They're both professionals who're used to seeing their names in print. But I can't guarantee they're still in possession of the objects. I'll ask."

"I'd prefer to do it myself. I don't want to arouse any suspicion. If you intervene, they might get the impression that I'm trying to sell. I want to be as discreet as possible. Furthermore, I don't want any middlemen trying to take advantage of me. My father trusted you, but at this point, we're not that well acquainted. It's my hope that over time we can develop the same kind of working relationship."

Marion nervously tapped her pen. He made a timid attempt to resist.

"You know the importance of professional confidentiality. I cannot divulge the names of the buyers without their consent."

Marion was silent, waiting for the man to be uncomfortable enough to cede ground. It didn't take long.

"One of the buyers is an appraiser who works with us regularly. He wasn't particularly attached to the piece, so he could have sold it. His name's Laurent Duverger. The second buyer was Alain Ozenberg, an antiques dealer." Mr. Rambert reeled off their names so quickly and quietly, Marion would have had to ask him to repeat them if she didn't know exactly who they were. "You'll have to forgive me for keeping the third buyer's identity a secret. This one is a special case—one of our more important clients and highly sensitive. But don't worry. This person will agree eventually. Actually, I think the buyer will be flattered."

What was most obvious to Marion was that Mr. Rambert didn't seem to be aware of Chartier's death. He was also trying to maintain his connection with her. Nonetheless, she had her information now and was seething at Duverger. If he still owned the sculpture, he had what he needed to be an unavoidable obstacle.

"Which piece did Laurent Duverger buy? Do you remember?" she asked.

"Yes, it was a jaguar. A magnificent piece."

"One more question, and I won't take up any more of your time."

"I've got plenty of time."

"Did my father know the buyers' names?"

"He was in the room with me, and when it comes to gamesmanship, your father was a master. I got the impression that he intuitively knew who would buy the pieces. He looked happier about the buyers than the prices the items fetched."

"That seems strange, doesn't it?"

"The word 'strange' was used a lot with your father."

Marion arranged a meeting for the following week and hung up. She was furious.

"That son of a bitch!" she yelled. "Duverger was screwing with me! Sending me cryptic messages through Gaudin! If he thinks he's going to steer me off course by playing puppet master, he's got another thing coming, They're all twisted, incapable of going through life without lying and manipulating. My father was exactly like the others—hiding the owners' names from me when he knew them all! What was the point? If it's because he liked scavenger hunts—damn, I'm too old for this!"

She was flipping through the articles left by Bruno, when Sophie put her head through the door. "Combes is here to see you."

"We don't have an appointment. Tell him I'm busy," she said, looking up to see the detective taking Sophie's place in the doorway.

"Marion, when were you going to tell me?"

Marion glanced at her bag by the door, which still had the sculpture in it, then looked back at Combes and put on a gracious smile.

"Tell you what, Didier?"

"About Magni. I'm investigating a major pre-Columbian piece of artwork that once belonged to the man, and you don't think it would interest me to know that you've just inherited his entire collection? Now I understand why you were so tense. What else aren't you telling me?"

Marion was at a loss for words. "I should have just assumed that everyone knows," she told herself. "What do I do now? I can't possibly tell him I also have the figure he's looking for."

"Well?"

"Listen, Didier, it's been a lot for me to take in. The man abandoned me as a child."

They looked at each other for a minute. Then Marion started shuffling through the papers on the desk. "I was just going through some articles about his death. Want to look them over with me?"

He made a face, stepped into the office, pulled up a chair, and picked up a newspaper.

"Look at this, from *La Prensa*. A daily Peruvian newspaper, I assume. A short death notice. 'A Frenchman by the name of Edmond Magni has died in Pacaipampa,'" Combes said after a few minutes.

"Didier, I didn't know you could read Spanish."

"There are quite a few things that you don't know about me, Marion."

"Pacaipampa, Pacaipampa," Marion repeated. "It's got a melodious ring to it." It sounded light and ethereal. What a strange place to die.

This was the first time she had seen the precise location of her father's death. The French journalists and her attorney had only mentioned some remote town in the Andes, probably because it sounded mysterious and in keeping with his image as pope of the art world.

Marion woke up the computer and typed in "Pacaipampa." It took a few seconds for the map to come up on the screen.

"It's in northern Peru, bordering Ecuador, some fifty miles from the Piura region," she said, thinking that was where the sculptures had been found. It wasn't far from Las Lomas, either, and its necropolis, the one Chris had talked about.

Questions raced through Marion's brain. Was Chris right? Had the sculptures come from Las Lomas? Why hadn't Pacaipampa shown up anywhere else? Had the name of the village been covered up to avoid any association with the pillaging of the necropolis?

Marion grabbed the newspaper out of the detective's hands and anxiously flipped through the rest of it. Its yellowed pages made it look older than it actually was. According to the date, it had been printed barely three years earlier.

Meanwhile, Combes started reading the famous American interview with Magni out loud.

"All collectors experience the high of acquisition, whether it's unexpected or longed-for. But the thrilling acquisition—the acquisition that electrifies the mind and body—is rare. It might happen just once in a lifetime. Perhaps the item is too expensive, or it's too hard to obtain. Very few men are willing to risk it all on an object they believe in, despite the consequences."

Marion struggled to control her breathing. She had accused her father of being calculating and Machiavellian. She had judged him for his ridiculous and distrustful behavior. But after concealing a sculpture from the police and sleeping with their scapegoat, that statement sounded frightfully relatable.

She watched Combes as he continued to read, hoping her discomfort didn't show, while questions bounced around in her head: "I'm risking it all, but for what? Money? A challenge? To find out about my father and his past? To recognize myself as Magni's daughter, envied and desired, no longer a scared and lonely little creature who thought she'd never measure up?"

There was so much elation and intoxication in this realization, Marion let herself run with it. But what about Magni? Had he ever questioned it all: his reputation, his beliefs, his lifestyle?

Marion understood now that he had been capable of doing anything. Organizing grave-robbing networks? So what? This illicit trade had been justified for many years. Why couldn't she do the same? The raids allowed thousands of impoverished families to stay alive. Few works of pre-Columbian art were acquired in a legitimate way. Museums were full of objects from Egyptian, Greek, Roman, and Etruscan civilizations. They needed to be preserved. And Peru certainly didn't have the means to preserve its heritage. Just a day ago, she would have rebelled against this kind of litany. But now the situation had changed. She saw the big picture. If she wanted the inheritance and was willing to accept the consequences, she would have to be swift and cynical. Avoiding culpability seemed so simple, she wondered whether the real problem with these sculptures was the fact that they had been plundered. Maybe that wasn't why people were killing each other. The question posed by Didier Combes remained unanswered: what was so important about the warrior and its companion pieces that people were willing to kill for them?

Instinctively, Marion glanced at her bag. It was sitting by the door of Bruno's office, and the sculpture was still in it. She didn't know what to do with it. She didn't want to leave it at SearchArt or at her place. But she couldn't keep carrying it around. She did have one idea—Chris. His lab had tons of boxes that nobody ever opened.

Combes had looked up from his reading and was watching her tap the desk with her pen.

"They all say the same thing," she said. "It seems he died of a heart attack. There are no details other than what the Peruvian paper printed: the name of the town where he died."

"Why don't you google it?" Combes said.

Marion focused on him for a minute. "Didier, what's happening to you? Suggesting I actually use technology for something."

"Yeah, you have to go with the times."

Bruno's computer was still on. Marion typed the words "Prensa," "Magni," and "Pacaipampa." Only two articles came up, each one no more than a few lines.

"It's hard to believe that no reporters ever looked into Magni's death. A wealthy white Frenchman hungry for pre-Columbian treasures had died under mysterious circumstances in a remote Peruvian town. Now that's a story."

Spotting the name of the mayor in one of the items, she changed her search, replacing the name of the Peruvian paper with "Julio Gomez," followed by "Pacaipampa" and "Magni." A single entry corresponded. It had been published by an even smaller publication. The date of the article was October 10 of the previous year. She started reading.

"Well, what do you know. A reporter interviewed the mayor. Edmond Magni had been known throughout the village for his sexual activities with young indigenous women. He had bought a house near a cemetery, where he lived a depraved life with total impunity. It was said that he paid the families handsomely in exchange for their daughters and their silence."

"He just gets better and better, doesn't he?"

"What a sick bastard. What made him such a monster?"

"Is there more in the article?"

"It says he died in the arms of one of the women. The authorities hushed up the death and said it was just a heart attack. But the woman claimed that an emerald-encrusted figure found beside the bed had cast a curse."

"How interesting," Combes said. "Those emerald-encrusted figures seem to be popping up all over the place."

"No trace of the sculpture was ever found. Do you think he was murdered because of this other sculpture?"

"Why didn't the story traveled further and make it to other papers or investigating authorities?"

"Do you think there were political or diplomatic reasons to keep the circumstances of his death hushed up? Or influential people trying to keep his vices a secret to protect his name?"

"I don't know, but in any case, it does bring us full circle," Didier said, placing a catalog in front of her, open to the warrior. "There's the figure I'm looking for. Have you learned anything else about it?"

Marion had all but stopped breathing as she took the catalog in her hands and focused on the artifact. She couldn't look at Combes. She couldn't speak.

"Marion? Are you there? Do you know anything about the warrior?"

She looked up at him just as the phone rang.

"It's for you," Sophie curtly informed her before hanging up.

No sooner had she taken the call than Chris started blurting out words she had trouble understanding—he was almost shrieking. He had left a dozen messages on her cell phone. Had she turned it off? He was very worried. Someone was following him. He was sure of it. He had called the cops, bought a burner phone. Combes had gotten back to him. He seemed to be putting the pieces together.

"Come to the office," she said to cut him short. Then she turned to the detective. "Didier, I have work to do now."

Combes took the catalog back, watching her closely. "Yes, of course. Let me remind you that this is a homicide investigation, and I need whatever you can find on that sculpture as soon as possible." He turned and left.

Marion didn't even have time to let out a sigh of relief before the door opened again and Sophie came storming in.

"There's a man out there for you," she sputtered. "He's weird-looking. Dressed like a bellhop and as big as the Hulk. He stopped by early this morning, and he's here again now. He says he's not leaving until he speaks with you. What do I do? He's creeping me out."

Sophie looked at her and then the mess of documents in front of her. Marion sighed and got up.

"Bring him in."

On her way out, Sophie stopped just short of the door. She turned around. "You're all going to make me go crazy," she said. She returned a few seconds later to introduce a man in a dark-gray suit. Marion thought he had the bearing of a servant, but considering his size, it was possible that he was in a more dangerous line of work.

"Mrs. Romarel would like to meet with you," he said.

Romarel… The name didn't ring a bell. She motioned to Sophie to leave.

"She could have called to arrange an appointment. That would have saved you the trouble of coming here for nothing," Marion responded.

"Mrs. Romarel would like to meet with you," he repeated. "I'm to drive you to her."

"Right this second? I can't. Give me her number. I'll call her when I can."

"I'll wait as long as you'd like."

The chauffeur seemed nailed to the floor, determined not to budge an inch. Marion stared at him. She didn't know what to think. Was the guy crazy? Was he in the wrong place?

Eventually she said, "I'm sorry, but I don't know this woman."

The man's eyes widened, and for a second, Marion had the impression that he, too, wondered if he was in the middle of a poorly scripted play.

"You are Marion Spicer, aren't you?"

She nodded.

"You didn't receive a call from the estate attorney?"

"What attorney?"

"You are Edmond Magni's daughter, aren't you?" he continued with a hint of concern in his voice.

"Yes."

"The attorney didn't tell you anything?"

"About what?" she asked, growing tired of his game-playing.

"Mrs. Romarel was your father's mistress," he whispered, looking down and apparently hesitant to disclose other people's business.

Her father's mistress? Marion had totally forgotten about the woman. Yes, the attorney had mentioned her. She had left Paris without giving anyone a forwarding address. He thought the chances of finding her were slim to none. This was exactly what she needed on what was already the world's weirdest day.

"I can't leave work right now."

"I'll wait."

"I have at least two hours of work to do, probably more. I'd prefer to meet with her another day."

"I'll wait."

This guy wasn't going to give up. Whatever Mrs. Romarel wanted to talk about, it had to be pretty important.

"By all means, if you've got time to kill," she finally conceded. "Make yourself comfortable in the waiting area. Sophie will get you a cup of coffee."

16

"Thank God you're here, Chris. I don't think I've ever experienced a messier, more chaotic, confusing, and out-of-control day in my life," Marion said. She proceeded to explain to him about Mrs. Romarel and her chauffeur, Didier Combes, and La Medici expecting a full report. Then she mentioned the warrior.

Leaning against a wall in Bruno's office, Chris looked her up and down. "Have you gone completely insane?"

Marion was standing in front of him, stone-faced.

"Someone's been murdered, Marion. You have to hand the sculpture over to the police."

"No way. If I do that, I can say good-bye to my inheritance."

"Your inheritance? What the hell are you talking about? You could be facing a prison sentence."

"I'm just borrowing it for a week or two."

"It's stolen goods, Marion. You'll be sentenced to jail time and charged with a fine so big, you'll be paying it off for the rest of your life. But I'm wasting my breath. You already know all of this. What you may not be aware of is this: that cop—Didier Combes—is chasing after you, and he's gaining ground fast, very fast. Just yesterday he faxed me pictures of your sculptures. Photocopies from a fancy catalog with handwritten annotations of the buyers' names. Apparently he didn't tell you everything."

"What do you think he's after?"

"An analysis of authentication."

"That's not what I'm asking. What do you think his motives are?"

"I'm not a psychic, Marion."

"Do you plan to help him?"

"There's no point in resisting. The analysis won't tell him anything new. But it won't be long before he uncovers even more information. You know the reputation he's got. He's a bloodhound. A bloodhound with a pit bull trap."

"Let's not get carried away, Chris. Didier and I work together. You know that. In fact, he was just here. He knows I'm Magni's daughter, but that's all. I'll tell him the truth eventually, but not until I find all the sculptures. Just hear me out, please. Magni knew who bought them. Why would he keep that from me? That's what I need to know."

"You can't try to justify the unjustifiable."

"I'm convinced he wants me to crack this mystery."

"That's ridiculous! What the hell's gotten into you?"

"I wish I knew! This is bigger than me." Marion paused before continuing. "I'm not going to abandon this collection or my inheritance. Weren't you the one who was just telling me the other day that millions of euros were worth a few sacrifices?"

"Finally. At least you're admitting the truth. It all comes down to money. It's changed the honest woman I knew."

"You're oversimplifying. It's more than the money. For the first time in my life, I feel like I'm actually living. Years ago I chose a quiet life for myself. That's what I wanted. And I stuck with my decision until last week. After what happened at the pool, I could have given up completely. But again, you were the one who told me that people who don't go after their dreams are cowards. And well, I don't know exactly what dream I'm pursuing, but it's there, and it's powerful."

"You're twisting my words."

Chris had planted himself next to a window. He was staring at the silhouette of a distant construction crane. The fog made it look iridescent.

"You'll help me, right?" Marion threw out.

There was silence for a moment. "I'm on your side," he finally said. "But I'm having some serious misgivings. I don't like it that you've gotten us into this mess."

"You can stop here and now if that's what you want."

Chris folded his arms and shot her an angry look. Marion realized that she could be losing her best friend.

"You win, Marion. I can't let you handle this thing all by yourself. I just can't. Call it loyalty, or pride, or stupidity. I'm in. What would you like me to do?"

"We have to find a place to stash the warrior."

"What? You have the warrior on you? What else don't I know, Marion? Okay—forget I asked. Just give the thing to me."

"Where will you hide it?"

"At my mom's place."

"Your mother's place? I thought we should hide it at your lab."

"No, not a good choice. There are too many people during the day and nobody at night. Anybody could steal it. But my mom makes jewelry. Remember? She's got all sorts of boxes. But I need to stress this, though: I'm being followed."

Marion tensed. While worrying about her own vulnerability, she had neglected to consider Chris's.

"Are you absolutely sure of that?"

"Sure of it? I've never spotted anyone, but I still feel this presence lurking behind me. I'm not dismissing it anymore or telling myself that it's all in my imagination. Someone is following me. But why me? And wouldn't it mean that you're being tailed too?"

Without answering, Marion cracked open the door to Bruno's office and checked to see if Romarel's chauffeur was still waiting. Sure enough, he was sitting in the reception area, just behind Sophie, who looked as stiff as a board.

"So? What did you decide?" Chris fired. "Are you giving it to me?"

"I have another idea. We'll meet tonight at your mom's place. I'll bring the sculpture. I'll make sure Romarel's chauffeur drives me."

"Do you think you can trust this guy? And even if you can trust him, do you think he'll make any difference if you're being tailed?"

She shot him an unequivocal look.

"Okay. I give up. You bring it."

He was right. The chauffeur was no insurance. But Marion intended to be the one to take the blame if anything went wrong. She didn't want to put her friend in that position.

Chris started to leave but stopped. "Please be careful, Marion. This is serious stuff. Think it over some more. You don't actually believe this sculpture just randomly fell into your lap, do you? Someone could have given you a little help. You got your inheritance, then two days later a guy was murdered. His sculpture got stolen, and it wound up with you. You could get nailed as an accomplice to murder!"

She just nodded. It was too late to turn back.

Once alone, Marion began skimming through the pages of an auction catalog. She didn't want to think about it or analyze it anymore. Then, making a split-second decision, she threw on her coat, grabbed her bag, and left like a bat out of hell. When he spotted his charge darting down the hallway, Romarel's chauffeur rose to his feet.

"Are we leaving?" he shouted as he headed toward the exit.

With a tweak or two, it could have been Sophie's parting shot.

"So you're leaving me by myself again!"

17

Jacqueline de Romarel had opened the door to Marion and let her in, but she wasn't even looking at her guest. She was staring absently at a Neapolitan painting in the next room, as though she wasn't aware of Marion's presence. Only the hum of the furnace broke the silence. Marion didn't know exactly what to do. Say something to disrupt the spell? Wait for Romarel to speak?

It was hard to determine the woman's age. Sixty-five? Seventy-five? Her red hair was fixed in place with a gel as thick as plaster. She had a peach-fuzz mustache and was wearing lip liner, smudged eye shadow, and powder. Marion tried not to stare but couldn't help herself. Romarel's skimpy dress revealed her saggy breasts and loose skin. Yet she was also wearing a silk scarf to hide her neck wrinkles. Her arms were toothpick thin, and her torso was pitifully gaunt. And this made her legs seem all the more shocking. They looked like two hefty barrels.

"My father must have been blind to have slept with this woman," Marion said to herself. Still, she had beautiful hazel eyes, and there was something intriguing about her—something simultaneously harrowing, ridiculous, and magnificent, like a *commedia dell'arte* performance.

"Let's have a seat in the other room," Romarel suggested, finally coming alive. She pointed her cane to a door on the right. "I hope it's not too hot for you. I spend a fortune heating this place. I keep it at a constant eighty degrees all year, day and night. For me the seasons are all one in the same. Ever since I've been forced to stay inside they've lost meaning."

Marion watched as the stooped woman started inching, crablike, toward the room she had indicated. Once at the doorway she stopped Marion, blocking her with her arm. Romarel slowly turned to a kitchen cart, opened a photo album on top of it, took out a picture, and handed it to Marion. It was a portrait of a beautiful odalisque stretched out on a cruise ship's lounge chair. She was unrecognizable. Maybe Magni wasn't so blind after all.

"That was me," Romarel said.

Marion heard the anger in the woman's voice. She felt like leaving then and there. She was wasting her time.

"Do you have a picture of him?"

For the first time, Romarel's eyes met Marion's.

"I'm sorry."

Romarel closed the album and started making her way into the sitting room, with Marion close behind. On the far side of the room, an indoor greenhouse containing tropical plants created an array of shadows on the wall.

"What do you know about him?" Romarel asked as she continued her labored trek.

"Nothing."

"Not even about his childhood?"

"No."

The old woman dropped into an armchair and nodded to another chair. Marion sat down. Romarel was breathing heavily, and her hands were shaking.

"In order to understand, you have to be on the inside," she said once she had stopped panting. "But you—you're on the outside. You'll never get anywhere without me."

Her tone was as sharp as a knife. Jacqueline de Romarel was not a likeable person, and she made no effort to be one.

"Do you know about the will?"

Romarel interrupted her with a wave of the hand.

"You're aware of how your father kept a tight fist on his collection. What you don't know is that he also kept all of his paperwork. Magni didn't throw anything away. Bills, gift certificates, letters, bank statements... He kept it in his tomb room. I'm sure you never saw it."

Marion shook her head.

"It's a room whose walls were lined with cardboard boxes—all identical. They were labeled by year. That's how he organized his documents. He'd keep everything in his office until the year ended, and then, into the tomb room it would all go, in its own neatly labeled box. Apparently he had some idea of when he would die, because he had all the boxes, including the one for the year that's not yet finished, delivered to my home. Some stunt—as if I wanted them!"

"Was it a joke?"

"Yes, a prank. That's how I heard about you—from the estate attorney. And Fabien, my chauffeur, has been looking for you ever since. But you were an elusive target."

Marion shifted in her seat.

"I was on the outside too. I hoped he'd fall in love with me eventually. How deluded I was. I never could have imagined the power his objects held over him and just how far they had removed him from the rest of the world."

Jacqueline de Romarel fell silent, and Marion was hesitant to pick up the conversation. She was clearly a bitter woman, having stewed in her disappointments for many years. Nothing Marion could say would change any of that.

Romarel started talking again. Her strained voice was barely a whisper, and Marion had to lean forward to hear. "Try one-upping a seductive mask or an alluring alabaster sculpture," she said. "It can't be done. Those mistresses are much more tantalizing than the real thing. You lust for them but never manage to unlock their mysteries. Who created them? Who were they created for? It was their well-guarded secrets that fascinated Edmond. And, in the end, they were much easier to live with than a real woman. After all, what sculpture would argue, contradict, or cause doubts?"

"That didn't stop him from living with you."

"But look what it cost me! I had to accept the fact that Edmond would touch them, stare at them lovingly, and wake up in the middle of the night screaming, 'I want her, I want her!'"

The regrets and loneliness pouring out of her host washed over Marion. Feeling dispirited, she began rubbing the fingers of one hand over the palm of her other hand. Why torture her with my questions, Marion wondered, torn between her reluctance to poke at old wounds and the desire to know more about her father. What good would it do?

As if she had read her thoughts, Jacqueline de Romarel fixed Marion in her gaze. "I wouldn't want you spending your best years chasing after him like

I did. I did everything I could to understand who he was. Learn from my mistakes."

"I don't understand where his fortune came from," Marion said, intent now on staunching the flow of melancholy.

"From his father's father," Romarel answered. "He left on a cargo ship with nothing and come back with a full hold. He founded a cotton business in Africa. It was successful enough to support several idle generations."

"The attorney didn't say anything about that."

"Edmond went through it all shortly after we parted ways."

"Why?"

"I wasn't there anymore to pay for his coveted pieces. He used his inheritance."

"All that time, you agreed to—"

Jacqueline de Romarel nodded.

"Our family had money, as well," she said.

"You could have said no."

The old woman sighed. "I didn't want to lose him."

"He wasn't always like that," Marion said, thinking of her mother. She had hung onto him with no money of her own.

"Maybe we should start from the beginning," Romarel suggested. "That's the key to it all."

She propped her legs up on a gilded-wood footrest, prepared to deliver a long requiem.

"It all started with his father's death. The poor man killed himself. He committed the grim act by a river smack in the middle of his property. He blew his head off with a shotgun. Edmond was the one who found him. A terrible thing for any child, but especially a keenly impressionable one like Edmond. You see, Edmond was born with an artistic gift. When he was no more than ten, his father built a studio for him and made sure he had the best materials. Edmond spent days sculpting in that studio. A child with his talent couldn't dream of a more extraordinary playground. So you can imagine his devastation when his widowed mother got rid of everything and closed the studio. She didn't want him to become an artist. She had other plans for him. But what could he do to oppose her? He dealt with his feelings by becoming a collector. He started bringing home broken rulers, pencil stubs, plastic bags, pieces of soap… Whatever he could get his hands on."

Romarel cleared her throat and looked into the distance.

"And then one day he discovered a chiseled-ivory skull. He was thirteen. That was the start of his quest. First it was skulls and bones and then those notorious mortuary sculptures. His mother paid for them. By this time she regretted destroying his studio and was willing to do anything to get her son to quit hoarding trash. But all that she managed to do was transfer Edmond's obsession to more valuable objects. He was desperately trying to fill the emptiness inside himself, and she couldn't change that."

Romarel stopped talking. "Pour me some water," she ordered. "There, on the table."

Marion got up and walked over to the heavy crystal carafe. As she started filling the glass, she lost her grip on the pitcher. She managed to regain her hold before it fell to the floor.

"He was just as clumsy as you, which is odd, because he was so gifted with his hands. And there's something else. I've been watching you since you got here. You have the same tic. When he was nervous or preoccupied he'd start drawing on the palm of his hand. Not with a pen, but with his finger."

A tic that connected them? The mention of it seemed to suck Romarel into a solitary daydream. She sipped her water with an absent look on her face. The old woman rested her head on the back of the chair and finally picked up the story again.

"If he had been an introspective man, he might have realized what he was doing and perhaps freed himself from his inner demons. But he was driven by his subconscious. Do you know what I think?"

The old woman lowered her voice as though she were about to reveal an incredible secret. "Those objects gave him proof that death didn't mean the end of existence. They were silent witnesses to his father's immortality. And his own immortality too, of course. Those objects were the only things that wouldn't abandon him. He'd abandon them, throw them into that basement morgue of his, but they were always there. In the end, they were all disappointments, just like I was. He'd bring one home, convinced that it would make him feel whole. But it wouldn't last long. Once the piece was in his hands, he'd lose interest. Into the cellar it would go, having lost all its magical powers, and he would start again. The next object had to be even more beautiful, rarer than the one before it. It was like a drug. He had to up the dosage each time to feel the drug's calming effects. That was all he thought about and talked about. He'd go through catalogs at all hours of the day and night. And sadly, the little boy who was lonely and isolated grew into a man who cut himself off from other people, ensuring that he was just as lonely and isolated."

Marion looked on dispassionately. What crap. He should have gone to see a shrink.

"As the years passed, and Magni became more selective, he began to make a name for himself. Eventually he became a tour de force. Everyone was jealous of his collection, even though nobody had ever laid eyes on it. He was a mythic figure in the art world. But I knew what he was. He was a sick man. I should have helped him instead of engaging in his perverted game. But I wanted him to see me, love me. I was so stupid. He only wanted me when I made it worth his while."

"You could have left once you realized what he was doing."

"That meant I'd have to admit my failure in getting him to love me. I couldn't do that. I stayed, but I changed my strategy. It was my turn to be his obsession."

Somewhere in the apartment, a clock started chiming. Jacqueline de Romarel was quiet and alert. Marion counted the chimes. It was already four o'clock.

"Where was I?" the old woman asked when the chiming stopped.

"You wanted to become his obsession."

"Ah yes… I started by insisting that I see every piece he wanted to acquire. After all, it was my money. I knew he wanted to go alone to the auction houses, antique shops, private showings, and flea markets, so I'd insist on accompanying him. And the night before I was supposed to give him the money to buy a piece, I'd wake him up and tell him that I'd changed my mind. I'd say it wasn't a good idea. I'd been spending too much, or my sister needed to borrow some cash. I was scared of him, but it was also exciting to see him suppress his anger and swallow his pride and then grovel at my feet. I liked that. He told me things I wanted to hear. And every time I'd end up giving in."

Marion was staring at Romarel, perfectly attentive to her sad disclosure. She wanted to understand what it was that made a woman so desperate. Had her mother stripped herself bare as well, become so overwhelmed by love and ego that she went insane? And her disgust, her visceral hatred for primitive art—was that her only awareness of how she had debased herself? What did these two women have in common?

"The only instruments of pleasure I had left were my tricks and schemes," Romarel continued. Her face looked peaceful now, as though telling her story was bringing relief. "And that's a slippery slope to hell. I reached a point where I didn't think I had a choice. I decided that I would take every piece he desired away from him. I made Fabien buy them first. But Edmond didn't bat an eye. No fretting, no questions. Nothing. I thought it was a sort of disengagement. A road to rehabilitation. I never imagined how diabolical he was. As it turned out, I was merely buying his bait. He was secretly indulging in other pieces."

"With what money?"

Jacqueline de Romarel shrugged.

"His own. Well, someone else's… I realized he was leading a double life when I started going through his things. How could I go that far—waiting for the moment when I could slip my hand inside his pockets or feel the inner lining of his coat? I was obsessed with a single goal: finding a receipt or credit-card statement that would prove there was an intruder. I was the wife who follows her husband to the place where he trysts with his new lover. Jealousy is most certainly a madness that drives you to destruction—destruction of yourself, the other person, or both of you. Someone always loses. And so one morning Edmond showed me how I had destroyed him."

Jacqueline de Romarel buried her face in her hands. Marion knew she should get up and comfort her. But she couldn't. Did she even want to hear the rest?

"He gashed his face," Romarel said, pulling herself together. "Three swipes with a razor blade across his right cheek. Just like that. Without any warning. He just gave me a cruel and arrogant little smile before his skin disappeared beneath a gush of blood. We were in the bathroom. There were mirrors on every wall, and they reflected his bloody face over and over. My head was spinning. I fainted, and when I came to he was gone. He never came back. In that one act he showed me what my compulsion to possess him had reduced him to."

Jacqueline de Romarel shot Marion a wounded look.

"You never tried to see him again?"

"No. Strange, isn't it? After spending so many years sucking the smallest bit of love out of him, I let him run off. The thing is, I felt free. No more chains, no more limitations, no more dread. I could finally live by myself and for myself. But eight months later I came down with lymphatic filariasis, a parasitic disease. I was treated, but not before developing elephantiasis. My legs swelled and became so deformed I couldn't stand looking at myself. Even if I could get around, I didn't want to go out anymore. I became a willing prisoner in my apartment."

Jacqueline de Romarel had been driven to a premature old age. Like Marion's mother, she was wasting away. They both had cut themselves off from society—one psychologically, the other physically. There was nothing in this world that either of them wanted enough to abandon their cocoons.

"But there's more."

Romarel's voice shook Marion from her thoughts. The eyes of her host suddenly sparkled, and her cheeks flushed with excitement.

"That's right. I also have my box of secrets."

Marion was silent, eager to find out where this woman was leading her now.

"Four sculptures."

"Four..."

"The ones I took from him, plus one more."

"It's one that I'm looking for, isn't it?" Marion said.

"Yes, shortly after our breakup I read in *The Drouot Gazette* that Magni would be putting some pieces from his collection up for auction. It was so unexpected. I couldn't miss out on such an event. I asked a merchant friend to buy everything for me. It would be like bringing a piece of Edmond back home. And it was my little attempt to exert a bit of control again. Unfortunately, I was able to buy just one piece. The others were too expensive."

With the authority of a confident matron she told Marion to get her trophies. "They're in the other room, in a chest to the left and toward the back. You can't miss it. It's a studded leather chest."

Marion rushed into the room and brought it back to Romarel. She started to open it. "No, don't do that," the old woman ordered. "I don't want to see them. Take them. One of those dreadful sculptures could be more valuable than Edmond let on. There are a lot of people who'd like me to sell them."

"Who?" Marion asked worriedly.

"Ozenberg, for one. He worked as a broker for me. He called my house just the other day. He wanted to know if I was ready to part with them. I was surprised. He usually sends his muscleman—once a year. The man always asks if I want to sell, but not with much conviction. It's more like he's just checking to make sure they were still here. But this call from Ozenberg was more… well, insistent."

A thousand and one thoughts raced through Marion's mind. Romarel was the person Alain Ozenberg had mentioned—the person clinging to her past. The infamous *Woman with Child* had to be inside that chest.

"Marion? Are you listening? You look so alarmed."

The touch of the old woman's cold fingers on her cheek was like an electric shock.

"Why would Alain need a muscleman?"

Romarel raised an eyebrow when Marion used Ozenberg's first name. "Don't let yourself get taken by the man's charm. He's not who you think he is."

Marion just looked at her. After a long silence, she asked, "What did the man he sent look like?"

"He's a skinny suit-wearing type, with intense blue-green eyes and a crooked nose."

Marion immediately made the connection. The man at the Louvre. The guy who was watching her.

"Have you noticed anything suspicious?"

"Fabien is here twenty-four-seven." Jacqueline de Romarel sank deeper into her chair. "And what more could happen to me now? My days are numbered."

18

"Whatever it takes, try to get some sleep. Cleanse your mind. No need to worry until tomorrow." Marion's inner mother wasn't working. She threw back the sheets and got up again.

Her own stream of words replaced her mother's. "Two of the three sculptures. I've got two of the three. In just two days."

Of the four objects Jacqueline de Romarel had given her, one of them was, indeed, a figurine she had been seeking: a woman with large emerald earrings. Her eyes were gazing into the distance as if she were more interested in some invisible spectacle than the child in her belly.

Marion was especially nervous when Jacqueline de Romarel's chauffeur dropped her off in front of the building where Chris's mother lived. With her sculptures under her arm and her thoughts battling one another, the tension had drained from her when she saw her friend.

"I'm so glad you're here." She wanted to tell him all about Romarel. She'd skip over the old woman's suspicions about Ozenberg. What was he about anyway?

"I'm glad I'm here too," Chris had answered, a little too quickly.

"Oh no, trouble at home?"

"Yeah, my wife and I had a big fight. Let's just say I'm more welcome here than at home. So I'm here for the night."

"So tell me about it." The fact that she could help her friend hash through his problems—instead of hers, for once—made Marion feel better. She really thought she might be able to sleep when she crawled into the extra bed in Beatrice Vallon's apartment an hour later.

It was a no-go. The room was too hot. She tried to crack open the window, but it wouldn't budge. She sat down on the bed, wondering if she should try to sleep again or turn on the light and look for something to read. Why had she agreed to spend the night here, anyway?

A door slammed somewhere in the apartment. Someone was opening a closet door and moving furniture around. She heard a chair scraping the floor. Two people were whispering. One of them was Chris. This wasn't the first night he had spent at his mother's. He was spending less and less time at his own place.

Marion fumbled in the dark for a good while before finding the switch on the bedside lamp. The bedroom suddenly turned green. Beatrice was obsessed with jewels. She had decorated her apartment in jewel tones, and each room had its own stone. This was the emerald room. Everything, from the fabric in the curtains and bedspread to the vases on the dresser, was green.

Unable to find anything to read and reluctant to disturb anyone in the next room, Marion stared at the sky on the other side of the window. Eventually it grew lighter, and the neon signs of the Montparnasse grew dimmer. The apartment was quiet, and it would have been safe to assume that everyone was sleeping if it weren't for the aroma of coffee. Marion threw on her jeans and shirt and padded barefoot into the kitchen.

In the semi-darkness, Marion saw that the floor was cluttered with boxes, and the table was covered with strange utensils. A round magnifying mirror with a long neck was attached to the windowsill. The shades were drawn, but a luminous beam was shining on the woman sitting with her back turned and her head tilted. It took Marion a few seconds to recognize Beatrice's curly hair. With her elbow resting on the table, the gemologist was in deep concentration. Afraid of interrupting her, Marion started backing up just as Chris put a hand on her shoulder. She let out a yelp.

"I couldn't stop her. She came back from the club an hour ago. And when she saw the emeralds, she just had to study them," he whispered.

Disoriented and tired, Marion looked from Chris in his T-shirt and boxers to his mother in a slinky gray dress before realizing that the *Woman with Child* was sitting right there on an improvised operating table.

"Pour me some coffee, please," she begged. "I won't survive without it."

Chris patted her sweetly on the shoulder and headed toward the back of the kitchen.

"I'd love another cup too, honey."

Beatrice had just lifted her head.

"This is surprising," she said to her son. "You would think these emeralds would be Colombian, but they're not."

Chris paused, coffee mug in midair, and shot Marion an inquisitive look, which she returned.

"Come look," Beatrice said without turning around.

Marion pulled out a chair, while Chris poured the coffee. Bringing the mugs to the table, he pulled out a chair for himself and sat down. Beatrice placed the sculpture in front of Marion. She guided the magnifying mirror over the right earring and then arranged the beam of light so that it shone on the emerald from the back. Marion watched Beatrice handle the instruments.

"Take the stone between your fingers and make it sparkle in the light," she instructed. "Now look through the magnifying glass to see the flaws in the stone. On the bottom there are fine lines that look like plant roots. Do you see them? Those are the famous jardins. They are actually tiny cracks that the emerald self-repairs through crystallization. Incredible, isn't it—a stone that can heal itself. And just above them you should see specks that are more or less brown. Those are flakes of mica."

All Marion could make out were shapeless dark spots and a jumble of needle-thin lines that looked like bamboo shoots.

"So can you see them?"

Beatrice slipped a hand underneath the thin strap of her dress and rubbed her shoulder while questioning Marion with her sage-green eyes. Marion replied with a skeptical pout.

Beatrice smiled. "Emeralds from Colombia don't have mica."

Marion held onto the woman's every word.

"They might contain pyrite or salt crystals, but no mica, which is rich in chromium. When emeralds are formed, they trap all sorts of elements from surrounding formations. If there's mica, it means a stone came from Brazil or Africa, most likely Zambia. Not Colombia."

"But remember, Latin America's indigenous cultures traded extensively centuries ago," Chris said.

"I wouldn't be worried if the stones came from Brazil," Beatrice said. "However, I would be concerned if they're from Zambia. And I'm leaning heavily toward that possibility. The blue-green color is as sharp as a Colombian emerald's, but there's a slight metallic aspect that's barely noticeable. Emeralds from Brazil are generally smaller, less than three carats, not like these ones here."

"You're absolutely sure about what you're saying?" Marion asked.

"I look at stones all day, Marion. I could certainly make a mistake. But this device doesn't."

Beatrice handed her an instrument equipped with an eyepiece.

"What's this?"

"It's a refractometer. It measures the amount of light that's bent, or refracted, in a gemstone. Every stone has its own refractive index. It's like a signature. It helps us identify the type of crystal, where it came from, and so on. Some gemstones have a single refractive index, while others have two. Emeralds have two, which means they refract light in two different directions. This often causes them to take on two distinct color patterns. I looked at the warrior's emeralds earlier, and I can tell you that they also contain mica—and chromium. But I'd suggest doing more tests to get definitive answers."

"I don't understand," Marion said, looking at Chris. "The *Woman with Child* sculpture went through your lab. And you didn't see anything?"

"We don't touch the stones."

"As I said, people make mistakes." Beatrice's magnifying glass was once again glued to an emerald. "Old techniques were used to cut these stones. Some of the work is rough. This all leads me to believe that the stones are ancient."

"But..."

"Call me if you want to have the stones analyzed at a lab," she said as she stood up. "I have to go now." Beatrice looked at her son. "I don't want to know what's going on at home, but try to mend things, honey. And get more sleep. You look a little pale."

She kissed her son's forehead. Chris rolled his eyes.

"A little pale!" he blurted as soon as she was out of earshot. "If she only knew what was going on. But she's too wrapped up in her own life. She's not interested in mine."

"Can you pour me another cup?" Marion asked, handing Chris her mug. "I'm so confused. I have no idea what all this means."

Chris didn't answer. He emptied the last of the coffee into his friend's mug. Then he sat down in his mother's spot and started inspecting the stones with the magnifying glass.

"Zambia..." Marion said softly, rubbing her temples.

"They could be from Brazil."

"Your mother was so sure of herself."

"Get them analyzed. Then we'll see."

"You don't believe her?"

"I do. But emeralds are tricky. I've seen people get fooled by synthetics."

"That's one of the things I'm having a hard time with. Why would you replace an authentic stone with another authentic stone? Doesn't it make more sense to replace an authentic stone with a fake?"

"It would seem that way, but it's not always the case," Chris said, still engrossed in his emerald inspection. "Maybe the original stones were missing, and the person who had the sculpture replaced them with another set of real stones to give the piece more value. I've seen that done with furniture. Collectors fiddle with furniture all the time by laying on the bronze."

Marion sipped her coffee and sighed.

"Only one person had his hands on both of these sculptures—my father. If all the emeralds are from the same place that would mean he was the one who switched them."

"Or someone tricked him."

Beatrice's comment about the stones was so spot-on, it was scary. The suspicion surrounding her father's questionable tactics, added to what she had heard about the unreliability of the lab results... Marion was suddenly struck with horrible doubt.

"What if they're fakes?"

"We'd be dealing with a real mastermind," Chris responded. He put down the magnifying glass and turned his chair to face Marion.

"You yourself told me last night that you had a strange feeling about them," Marion said. "Their stability and weight weren't right."

"I also said that I'd never held them before. These pieces speak for themselves, Marion. Look at the motifs on the child. They allude to cosmology—the sun, the moon, the stars, the sea. Not even the most talented forger in the world would venture to create such embellishments. Plus, there's so much life and character in these figures. An imitation imprisons life and freezes it in place."

Chris held her gaze. "Also, if they were stolen, they couldn't be imitations. That would be too big a stretch."

"I hope you're right."

"There's nothing wrong with these sculptures. The *Woman with Child* has gone through extensive lab tests already, and we didn't find anything abnormal. You're getting all worked up for nothing. At any rate, whether they're real or fake, what does it matter as far as your inheritance is concerned?"

"Are you really asking me that question?"

"Yes, I'm asking that question. And it's a perfectly reasonable one. Let's assume, for the sake of argument, that the sculptures are imitations. Sure, you might not be able to sell those two pieces, but you'd still come into your fortune. Right? The will stipulated that you acquire the pieces. End of story."

"But the stones."

"What about the stones? I just told you—they're not your problem." Chris was clearly becoming frustrated. "They've been handled by dozens of people, and no one's batted an eye. Take advantage of the situation. Just wing it like everyone else. Magni's name alone is enough to ensure that the sculptures are authentic. You couldn't dream of a better guarantee."

"I wonder! Look at us. You're trying to convince me that I shouldn't waste my time examining my suspicions. What if everyone else is thinking like you? What if other people have doubts but haven't said anything because they've been using Magni as their cover?"

"Where are you going with this, Marion?"

"What if he decided he was done? Done with the cheats. What if he wanted to show everyone his inadequacies and say, 'Figure this shit out for yourself. Don't count on me to cover your asses anymore.' He already suggested that at his infamous dinner party. Maybe he was fed up with serving as everyone's reference."

"He had an insatiable need for power."

"Chris—destruction is the ultimate act of power for someone who thinks he's God."

"You expect me to believe that he created fakes in the hope that someone would discover and expose his fraud—you, as it happens—as a way of ridiculing the industry and wreaking havoc?"

"Yes. First me, then everyone else. 'I bestow the shit storm on humanity.' We've been looking at this all wrong, Chris. I thought people were trying to stop me from finding the sculptures because they were little ticking bombs threatening Magni's reputation. That's probably half right. But if the sculptures are fakes, that changes everything. Magni would be like a horseman of the Apocalypse. He died, and the market died with him."

"Yes, I get it that he was a larger-than-life character, but he wasn't a man capable of devastating an entire market."

"All I know is that he scares the crap out of me, Chris. I've got a feeling of dread in the pit of my stomach. I hear the hooves coming toward us."

19

Didier Combes leafed through the catalogs on the melamine table, while René Joseph fingered a bronze statue.

"Ah, Mr. Duverger, there you are," Combes said as the man approached the appraiser walked over to the homicide detective and moved the statue out of his reach.

"Please, sir, don't touch. What can I do for you?"

"Didier Combes, white-collar crime, and this is René Joseph, with homicide."

"Homicide? How can I help you gentlemen?"

"Well, you no doubt know about Chartier. Rumors spread faster than the speed of light in your small world," Combes said.

"Yes, I had heard that he met with a rather unexpected death."

Joseph moved in closer to the man, crowding his personal space. "'Rather unexpected death,' I love it Didier. I'll remember to use the expression the next time I'm trying to describe a brutal murder and ritual disfigurement. What do you think?"

The two detectives turned and watched the blood drain from Duverger's face.

"What does this have to do with me?"

"Mr. Duverger, we'd like to know more about that jaguar you purchased at the Magni auction," Combes said.

Duverger put his hands behind his back and wandered over to one of the large display cabinets, eyeing it as if he were looking for dust. "Yes, a lovely piece. I sold it shortly afterward to an American buyer."

René Joseph smiled at the man. "Yep. That's what your secretary said too. She even e-mailed us the receipt. Funny, though, we couldn't find any trace of the buyer."

"I can't help you with that, sirs. You know the art business, full of people wanting to remain anonymous."

"How well did you know Edmond Magni?" Combes gave his partner a nod, indicated that he'd take over the questioning.

"Barely at all."

"Have you heard of a certain Alain Ozenberg?"

"Of course, he's well known in art circles, but we don't do any business together."

"How is the market reacting to Magni's collection potentially going on sale?"

"I haven't heard anything."

Combes moved away from the man and turned to Joseph. "What did I tell you, René. There's a code of silence in the art world."

"I'm guessing they settle their scores privately, too."

"No doubt. If I had one of those sculptures, I'd be worried about ending up like Chartier."

~ ~ ~

As soon as the detectives left, Duverger shouted at his secretary. "Pretend that I don't exist today. Got that?"

He grabbed his coat and headed to his car.

"Take me to Passy," he told his driver.

Duverger did have one of the three sculptures, and he knew now that he had a target on his back. But what made him furious was that he had taken the wrong route in tending to Marion. How could he have known that a mastermind would be pulling the strings, helping her and protecting her?

The appraiser stewed as he watched Paris go by through the window. He couldn't think of the warrior being in Marion's hands without getting the chills. Did she comprehend the stakes here? A massacre of the market—as well as his own demise. He hadn't sacrificed everything to watch his empire crumble.

Gaudin looked expressionless when he answered the door.

"Mr. Duverger. Please come in," he said, inviting the appraiser into the parlor, where Magni had hosted his dinner party. Images of that night flashed in Duverger's mind.

He turned to Gaudin without even waiting for an invitation to sit down. "I know what you've been up to. Nobody else is aware of the terms of Marion's inheritance. You're colluding with her to protect your turf. I know it. I used that shaman statue to warn you. Now I'm here for the direct approach. I could jeopardize Magni's integrity and reputation in a minute. But I'm not about to let everything get blown to pieces. You need to stop helping the girl. You're fooling yourself if you think you can control her. And don't think about coming after me the way you did with Chartier. I'm not the problem here, Marion is."

"What are you talking about?" Gaudin finally interjected. He denied the whole thing, repeating over and over that he wasn't involved. No, he hadn't masterminded Chartier's slaying. No, he hadn't helped Marion.

His denials confused the skeptical appraiser. Duverger had expected a much more cunning and less cooperative character.

Was he that good at hiding his cards? Gaudin couldn't have spent all those years so close to Magni without absorbing some of his lying, cheating, and trickery.

Duverger's eyes gravitated toward a beautiful bronze statue. He tried to silence his thoughts as he stared at the beauty: a pregnant woman with voluptuous curves and a delicate arched back. Joseph Erhardy. Yes, she had his signature style written all over her. He hadn't noticed this sculpture on his previous visit.

He brought his gaze back to the even-tempered Gaudin. He'd try another tactic.

"They're fakes."

"Fakes?"

"Yes, fakes. Perfect imitations. The same materials, the same traits, the same colors, the same shapes—fakes."

This was revenge enough for Duverger: seeing the personal assistant as he pictured the far-reaching effects of the scandal. He delighted in that brief moment of triumph, when Gaudin looked stupefied, as though he had to deconstruct the notion in order to comprehend it. Then Duverger realized the assistant knew exactly which sculptures were at play.

"That's impossible," Gaudin said, his tone perfectly flat.

"Those sculptures are a threat to the collection, Gaudin. They must not be out in the wild."

That would bring the man around. He was more loyal to Magni's museum than Magni himself.

"But scientists, specialists, technicians, and curators have looked at them, examined them. That can't be. There's one at the Louvre, for God's sake."

"Alas, it is. Magni was the reference. With his reputation, the curator certainly didn't look close enough. You'd be surprised how often that happens. They are top-notch forgeries. The craftsmanship is excellent."

"Marion would lose everything if she reported the fakes. Her entire collection would be tarnished. Have you told her?"

"Marion's a loner, a maverick. She lives in the moment. I could never trust her enough to conspire with her. She could go rogue too easily."

Duverger decided to skip to the chase.

"He was the one who sculpted them."

"Magni sculpted fakes? I don't believe so. No, that's impossible. What would be the point?"

"Good God, Gaudin, wake up!"

"But he could afford the real thing."

"You don't get it at all, do you?"

"Get what?"

"Magni was fed up. He had worked his whole life to become an unrivaled force. And he was. No one could stand in his way or question his choices. Eventually he got bored, Gaudin! He wanted to have fun, mix it up. And to that end, he was willing to present fakes as genuine and absolute paradigms."

"That's bullshit. Pseudo-psychology," Gaudin spat out. "Magni wouldn't have risked losing everything just for the sake of having a little fun."

"Are you fucking kidding me? Need I remind you of what he always said? 'Art is like pâté. You know instantly whether it's good or not. You don't need to understand how it's made to want it.' You heard him say that, right? He looked down on idlers—people who are incapable of forming their own opinions. Shit, Gaudin, surely you saw this coming. Magni couldn't have made a more blaring proclamation of contempt for our kind. He embraced Umberto Eco's dogma as his own—the 'absolute fake'—the fabrication of something better than the real thing—Las Vegas and Disneyland—to make people feel good and turn a big profit."

"He could have selected the ugliest sculpture out there and elevated it to an icon. Why would he resort to sculpting forgeries?" Gaudin argued, unwilling to admit the truth.

"You know I'm right."

Duverger stood up, ready to play hardball. He had just demolished Gaudin's house of cards, and now he needed to convince him that his viewpoint was valid. He walked around the couch, then stopped and looked the assistant in the eye.

"You're living in a bubble, an imaginary world. You'd rather feed your manservant convictions and deny reality. But the truth is knocking at your door. You can't escape it—the truth about Magni, his subversion, his harshness, his hatred for mankind, his violence, his cruelty. You really need to get that through your thick skull. He cheated you, took you for a ride."

"Do you have proof?"

Without saying a word, Duverger headed to his briefcase and took out a file.

"The Oxford laboratory confirmed his fraud," Duverger said, handing over the documents. In a quiet voice he added, "I wanted that sculpture. I wanted it because it had belonged to him. I, too, came face to face with my flaws."

"This is madness," Gaudin whispered. "Every piece passed the thermoluminescence test."

"Those tests aren't bulletproof. Magni knew their weaknesses and exploited them."

"How?"

"He exposed the fake pieces to ultraviolet light to age them. He knew the light would miss certain parts of the pieces, like nostrils and underarms. But he also knew that most labs don't test an entire object, and the tests aren't exhaustive. His method wasn't foolproof, but he was betting that the pieces would pass inspection. It's only because I insisted on a painstaking examination that Oxford discovered the truth."

Duverger wanted to be done with this. As Gaudin continued to examine the papers, the appraiser walked over to the bronze statue. He resisted an impulse to pick it up and touch the heavy breasts, delicate neck, and full hips. The assistant straightened up in his chair and shot him several nervous glances. "Look at that," Duverger said to himself. "He's like a jealous lover."

"If you think about it, Magni's scheme is diabolical," Duverger said, still admiring the bronze. "He calculated everything. And now, even from beyond the grave, he's taking aim at us—through his daughter. Are you listening to me, Gaudin? He wants to use his daughter to create so much suspicion, the market won't be able to do anything but collapse."

The room was completely silent.

"Hello? Cat still got your tongue? You do realize that trying to pass off an ordinary-looking piece wouldn't have satisfied him. He had to craft objects that looked priceless. You had your misgivings, didn't you? Don't tell me otherwise. I'd find that hard to believe."

Duverger didn't need an answer. Worry was written all over Gaudin's face. Yes, Magni's assistant had entertained his own doubts, but he had put them out of his mind. Now he had proof that his hunch was right all along.

"We have to keep any rumors from spreading," Gaudin whispered, handing the papers back.

"That's exactly why—" Duverger hesitated for a second. "Marion must be stopped. She'll lead us straight into a wall. You shouldn't have stopped my men at the pool."

Gaudin didn't respond.

"We have to decide. Eliminate the sculptures or eliminate Marion. We don't have a ton of options here."

~ ~ ~

A jolt of fear shot up the assistant's spine. So Duverger was the one behind the attack on Marion. And now the appraiser was trying to strike a bargain with him. But Duverger wasn't thinking. With those detectives poking around, making either Marion or the sculptures disappear would be like playing Russian roulette. Gaudin was finally beginning to see things clearly, and he was getting angry. He had been Magni's watchdog. He had tended to everything the man had asked him to do, and just a minute earlier he had proposed a cover-up. That was then. Now he wanted out of this mess. Preferably a way out that would allow him to take revenge on the employer who had put him in an untenable position. He would sabotage Magni's scheme.

"We have to inform the press. Tell them the objects are fakes," he said.

"Are you nuts? You want to mess with Magni?"

Duverger had his hand on the bronze. A clear attempt at intimidation. Gaudin was silent for a few moments, trying his best to avoid taking the bait.

"I want the same result as you," he finally said.

"You still don't get it."

"One day or another someone will find out, and they'll talk."

"You're not saying a word. Got it? Not a word!" the appraiser shouted, pointing his finger at Gaudin.

"Duverger, listen to me. It would be best to take control of the situation now, and cut out the cancer before it spreads."

"Because you believe in transparency? Is that your plan to help you sleep at night?"

Duverger was tensing up.

"A disclosure of this magnitude would have an unbelievable domino effect. Is that what you want?"

"We'd be taking a risk, yes. But the reaction might not be as dramatic as you fear. The media will feast on it for two or three days, and then they'll move on to something else."

"We're not taking the risk."

"You think taking out Marion will be more effective and make less noise than just coming clean? Think again. Murder her, and the reporters will come out in droves, and before you know it, they'll be all over Magni and the sculptures. You're going down a very treacherous path."

"Gaudin, she already has two pieces. That's all it takes to make her a threat."

"You're too scared to be thinking straight."

"There's good reason to be scared when you're dealing with a man who's as narrow-minded as you. Keep your mouth shut. That's all I'm asking. I'll take care of the rest."

"I will not stay quiet."

Gaudin barely had time to register the fury on Duverger's face. All he saw was the bronze woman raised above his head. He tried to shield himself from the blow, but his hands were too fragile a defense. Before his head exploded, he closed his eyes and imagined the warrior with emerald tears. Gaudin knew no one would shed any tears for him.

20

"I want to feel your breasts, Marion. I want to smell your hair. I want to be deep inside you, to taste your mouth, and your neck. I need to feel your breath, hear your screams."

After what seemed like an eternity of silence, Alain Ozenberg whispered, "Meet me, now."

Marion listened to the message on her voice mail one more time. It was blunt, racy, explicit, exciting, erotic, and surprising. How could she not respond to that? If only he knew. He was a force of nature shaking up so many feelings inside her. Something sharp and painful—the sense of losing herself. But also something new and precious: an awareness of excitement and sensitivity. It was incredible how she loved his passion, his way of breaking through a barrier separating two worlds: the wild and the refined. Incredible how she loved the way his voice changed when he caressed her body.

But no, something was off. His name was coming up too many times. What was his real connection to all this?

For now, the sculptures demanded her attention—and her involvement. Marion had gone home to change clothes before meeting with Laurent Duverger. Chris had given her tips for shooting holes in the appraiser's game. Her friend had done some additional analysis on the sculptures. They were definitely fakes.

A real murder over a replicated object, real fortunes paid for clones, real cops investigating the crime of receiving stolen duplicates, a real will and testament bequeathing imitations. That pretty much summed up Magni's legacy. Her father had given her nothing, nothing but chaos and ruin. And if she exposed the sculptures' true nature, she would have nothing.

Still under Ozenberg's influence, she was tempted to drop everything and cancel her meeting with Duverger. But she couldn't afford to lose any time. Combes was hot on her trail. If she wanted to claim all three sculptures, she would have to act fast. Once that was done, she'd be free to decide on the issue of selling.

Marion knew she was charging into the lion's den. But being aware of the dangers and moving ahead anyway gave her a rush. And that feeling, which she had already discovered with Ozenberg, was liberating. No longer a timid and scared little girl, she had the sense now that she could meet a threatening situation and master it. And so, on this afternoon, the challenge was dealing with Laurent Duverger.

He would wait for her at two o'clock at the Elsa photo gallery in the Verdeau Passage, where he was handling an appraisal. Marion was familiar with the area. Just five years earlier, the place had played a role in her professional life. It was there that she had met a collector who, moments after acquiring a photograph by Gustave Le Gray, had burned it right in front of her and the gallery owner. Two hundred thousand euros up in smoke without the slightest trace of guilt on the buyer's part. She had sworn on that day to never again interact with collectors. The irony of fate. She was now the heiress of the world's most famous collector.

~~~

As she approached the well-lit gallery with its large glass windows, she had no trouble making out owner Marc Chastagne conversing with Laurent Duverger. The place hadn't changed a bit over the years. It still catered to mainstream clients who liked everything out in the open, rather than the privileged few who were accustomed to viewing their prospective purchases in private rooms and secretive galleries. The art dealer barely deigned to greet Marion. Looking both excited and relieved to be ending his side of the conversation, Duverger drew her by the arm to a corner of the shop.

"Let's go get coffee—some place close by," he said in a tone that was welcoming—practically ecstatic. "I'll be back," he told the owner, who seemed to be trying his best to keep up a good front. His smile was friendly but tense.

"You have my sculpture, don't you?" Marion said as soon as they were seated. She didn't intend to dilly-dally or get bogged down in foreplay. She wanted to take the appraiser by surprise if that was still possible.

"Yes, I have it," he said as he nonchalantly removed his leather jacket.

A waiter carrying a silver tray came over to their table.

"Are you selling it?" Marion asked, keeping a tight grip on her victim, who immediately ordered a hot chocolate.

"No."

"Why not?"

"Don't you have the other two?"
~~~

"Why does that matter?" Marion was giving the direct tactic her all, while the man was hedging.

"We'll pretend you have them."

"Okay, let's say I have them."

"I will lend you mine for the time it takes you to testify that you, indeed, have all three."

Marion was panicking inside, but she wasn't about to let Duverger see it. She had no reason to trust him, and deep down she understood that he was hiding something.

"In exchange for what?" she asked at last.

"Afterward, you'll give me the two sculptures."

She suppressed a shiver, aware that she had to march straight in and lie without messing up. "They're worth a fortune—"

"That's not all," the appraiser interrupted. "I want exclusive rights to the appraisal."

"If I sell!"

"I'm not twisting your arm."

"It would be a sort of guardianship."

"Call it whatever you want."

"What about George Gaudin?"

"He won't have anything further to say in the matter."

"Why's that?"

"Because we'll sell the objects one at a time to avoid saturating the market. We have years of work ahead of us. And Gaudin will have all the time in the world to look at his clay figurines."

Marion could see the upside of this arrangement. She had no interest in business or finance. But there was a downside too. She didn't want to be connected to this man for life.

"Sell me your sculpture. Just name your price," she said in a final attempt to come out on top.

"You know very well… I have no interest in selling."

"Why do you want all of them?"

"They're part of an ensemble."

"What about the one from the Louvre?" she asked, wondering why the fifth piece, *The Tattooed Man,* was absent from this discussion, as well.

"It's out of play. It won't ever appear on the market again."

The precision of his response took her by surprise. Marion clutched her cup and brought it to her lips to gain some time. Duverger had done his homework. He knew, or at least suspected, that there was a problem with the sculptures, and she had only a few seconds to decide before making her move.

"Would they instill doubt regarding the rest of the collection?" Marion saw an instant reaction on the appraiser's face: a hint of panic in his eyes and tension in his jaw.

"You realize that your fortune doesn't depend on just you, don't you?"

"Same goes for your fortune. Without my silence…"

"Hence, a mutual understanding."

The appraiser was still using his as-few-words-as-possible strategy. Marion wanted to make sure she was following along. Was it Duverger's intent to quietly take the sculptures out of the picture because of their suspicious nature and the threat to the market that they posed? Was she ready to seal the deal?

"You were nothing to your father. Nothing but a cog in his power-hungry machine," the appraiser said, as if he needed to hit her with that reality to convince her to team up with him.

Marion took it on the chin. Hearing this come from someone else's mouth was really no shock. Her father had never extended himself to her. For her, he had been dead for a long time.

"There's still the collection," she said. "At least he's given me that. And I'll remain the sole owner. No guardianship and definitely not yours."

"So we are in agreement over the most important factor then?" he said, practically ecstatic.

"What is the most important factor, in your opinion?"

"Those sculptures never existed. Apparently I have more to lose than you do. But all things considered, it could be the reverse..."

"So you'll let me have your jaguar then?"

"Yes, I will lend it to you. And at the right time we'll destroy them."

"And what about the rest of the collection?"

"You will surely end up calling on me," Duverger responded, a smile returning to his face. "You see, I'm the best."

21

With Chris right behind her, Marion climbed the stairs to Magni's mansion two at a time. She was moving with the ease of a woman who thought she owned the world. She was prepared to tell Gaudin the truth and put him in his place for once and for all. But she'd be generous. She wouldn't kick him out. Not right away. After all, if she was going to be a permanent fixture here, what was the rush?

Just as she was about to push the doorbell, Marion heard a phone ringing inside the apartment. Gaudin wasn't picking up. He was usually home at this time of day. Marion didn't know why, but she had a feeling in the pit of her stomach. She looked at Chris. Seeing the worry on her face, he asked for the key and opened the door himself. The phone was still ringing, and the sound was lingering in the otherwise deadly still apartment. Gaudin wasn't there. And yet Marion felt someone was there. The place smelled of sweat: strong, rank, and sickening.

Marion cautiously stepped into the parlor. It was a wasteland: drawers on the floor, paintings yanked off the walls, armchairs knocked over, carpets rolled up…

But oddly, there was something methodical about the chaos. The place had been tossed, but nothing had been destroyed. No broken glass on the floor, no papers strewn about, no smashed lamps or vases. Once the paintings were hung again, the chairs were turned right-side-up, and the carpet was rolled back over the floor, the parlor would look the way it always had.

"Don't touch a thing," Chris instructed. His face had turned ghostly pale, and Marion, who assumed she was looking just as white, couldn't help but crack a nervous smile. His cautionary order sounded like something out of trashy horror movie.

Chris started inspecting the room, carefully avoiding the objects scattered on the floor. He lifted the curtain hanging over the cellar entrance and tried unsuccessfully to open the door. With an unsettled look on his face, he began examining the far side of the room. He approached the overturned sofa in front of the fireplace. Still at the entrance to the parlor, Marion was following him with her eyes. When her friend peered around the sofa and cried out, she rushed over.

Gaudin was lying in a pool of dark-red blood. He was curled in a fetal position, and his hands were shielding his head. His face, partially concealed by his fingers, was oozing blood clots and pus. His cheekbones and nose were smashed, making his open mouth look all the more grotesque. Placed triumphantly beside the torture victim's body was a bronze sculpture—a beautiful pregnant woman with voluptuous breasts and hips—which reinforced the macabre aesthetic.

Marion clutched Chris's arm. Her head was whirling, and her stomach was churning. They stumbled back to the door.

"Here, take my cell," she whispered, handing him her phone. "Call Combes, quick."

"Are you sure you want me to do this?"

"Call him," she ordered. "Tell him… Tell him we're waiting for him."

And with that, she ran out of the mansion and released her disgust, her incomprehension, and her disappointment over the wrought-iron railing.

~ ~ ~

How long had they been in Chris's car, clinging to each other in a stupor? Combes was taking an eternity. But when he knocked softly on the car window, she looked at the time and saw that only ten minutes had passed.

"Unlock the doors," the detective ordered. He slid into the backseat and didn't bother asking them how they were before laying everything out for them. "Okay, this is what we're doing. It won't be long before homicide shows up, and I don't want you to be seen here. We'll talk about all this first thing tomorrow morning."

Neither Chris nor Marion responded.

"Do you understand me? You cannot go home tonight. I'll be at this hotel tomorrow morning." Combes handed Marion a card. "Do not go home! Is that clear? You're in danger!"

Marion's eyes filled with tears, and her voice felt thick. "I threw up. Behind the stairs."

"Nothing else, though, right? You didn't touch anything?"

The two friends shook their heads, but Chris quickly corrected himself.

"The door leading to the cellar."

"Where's that?"

"In the main room, on the right."

"Nothing else—are you sure? Okay, let's get out of here. And try to get some rest. I'll be needing both of you."

~ ~ ~

The vinyl wallpaper with gigantic red petunias was peeling. The shabby drapes were threadbare, and the gray carpet was worn. But the huge and inviting bed in the middle of the room was covered with a fluffy white duvet and plush pillows. Fully dressed, Marion and Chris slipped under the covers. A sign in the lobby had informed them that each room was furnished with a brand-new American-style bed. And the hotel had delivered. The mattress had the lush feel of a featherbed from another era.

Finally, Marion and Chris felt safe. It didn't matter that a neon light was flashing outside their window or that noises were coming from the other side of the wall. The concierge, a friendly guy, seemed to have gotten specific instructions to take care of them. He told them he would be bringing up breakfast around six o'clock, and he would be available all night if they needed anything.

Marion, her hands behind her head, spent a long moment staring at the ceiling before turning to her friend.

"Let me handle Combes. Whatever you do, don't get involved."

She looked up at the ceiling again, torn between a compulsion to talk about the slaying and the need to digest the shock. Chris broke the silence.

"About these murders related to Magni. How come you and I have been able to escape? You were attacked, and then we were followed, but we're both still safe and sound."

"Magni made sure we were protected so we could carry out his plan." Marion had realized this shortly after her meeting with Duverger.

"You were nothing but a cog," he had said. "Magni used you."

"We should try to get some shut-eye," Marion suggested, even though she didn't think she'd be able to sleep.

"I can't. Maybe some whiskey would help." Chris jumped out of bed and headed straight to the mini-fridge.

He's going to overdo it, Marion thought as she watched him down the contents of one of the tiny bottles. That one emptied, he opened another and then another. When all the bottles were empty he crawled into bed again, turning his back to her.

"Good night," he muttered. Even facing the other way, he stank. Highly annoyed, Marion tried to push him out of bed. He didn't budge. She tossed and turned and finally put her pillow over her head to block the smell. She was just nodding off when someone knocked on the door. Marion tried to ignore it, but the person at the door knocked again, louder this time.

Marion finally got up and found herself face-to-face with a grinning Didier Combes, who was carrying a breakfast tray. The nerve of him, arriving unannounced at the crack of dawn. "I haven't had the chance to collect my wits yet."

The detective set the tray on the nightstand and poked Chris, who was still in a comatose-like slumber. He awoke with a start. "What's going on?" he shouted, jerking his head off the pillow.

"It's the moment of truth," the detective announced ambiguously.

Chris turned to Marion, who was quietly stirring her coffee. She gulped it down and poured herself another. It was watery and lukewarm, but it was doing the trick.

"We need some more," she told Combes.

"I thought you would. Another round is on its way."

Combes opened the drapes and sat down in a chair by the window. It was dark outside. Still groggy, Marion paced the room.

"May I smoke?" the detective asked, breaking the silence.

"No," Marion answered. She was nauseated. She walked over to the breakfast tray and picked up a slice of toast, hoping it would settle her stomach.

She finished the toast, and Combes started in. "What were you doing at Magni's place yesterday?" he asked.

"You mean my place?" she said, shooting him a defiant look.

Combes didn't waste a second. "It's not yours yet, unless you know something that I don't know."

"What do you want to know?"

"Why'd you bring him with you?" Combes asked, pointing his chin at Chris.

"Gaudin scared me."

"Why?"

"Because he was excluded from the inheritance."

"That's not a response."

"Is the coffee coming?" Marion asked.

"Why were you scared?" Combes pressed.

"I don't know. I don't know anymore, Didier. Nothing's making sense to me. I thought he had every reason to stop me or squeeze me out. My father's will had conditions. As long as I didn't recover the three sculptures, Gaudin could control the collection.

"Did you find them?"

"No."

"Come on, Marion. I need more. Who tried to drown you?"

"You know about the pool?"

"You should have told me. So who was it, then?"

"Can we take a break, Didier? I can't think straight, and my stomach hurts." She sat down on her floor, her back against the wall. She thought she could concentrate better with Chris out of her line of vision.

"We don't have time for a break, Marion. I don't think you understand the gravity of the situation. You'll have to be more talkative than this. I wasn't the one who discovered the body. Make a little effort. It could spare you some unpleasantness. I'll ask you one more time: who tried to drown you?"

"How do you expect me to know that? My disappearing from the picture serves nobody's purpose, except maybe Gaudin's, and he's gone now."

"What about Duverger? He has one of your sculptures."

"He's not the only one."

"Yes, but he's the only one suspected of murder."

"What do you mean?"

"We have several clues leading us to him. He's no doubt an excellent appraiser, but he's a poor murderer. He wiped down the weapon, but he left prints everywhere else."

"Duverger killed Chartier?"

"No, he killed Gaudin."

Marion shrank inside as she absorbed the news. So now she was colluding with a murderer.

"But why would he kill Gaudin?" she forced herself to ask, remembering how Duverger had apparently put the personal assistant entirely out of his mind when they met to negotiate their deal. There he was, all smiley, relaxed even. And he had just killed the man. Could you murder someone that easily? Would he have done the same to her if they hadn't struck a deal?

"Have you met with Duverger?" Combes started again, unwilling to give up.

"Yes."

"Marion," Chris cried out.

"He was trying to get in touch with me—"

A knock at the door. Combes practically jumped out of his chair to let the concierge in.

"I'm listening," he said, after tipping the concierge and setting down another tray.

"He entrusted SearchArt with finding a sculpture that had been stolen from him. It was at Magni's. I checked."

"Why would he do that?"

"He definitely wanted me to believe that he could pressure me."

"Do you have reason to think Duverger was blackmailing anyone?"

"How would I know? If my father wasn't such a mystery man, maybe I could tell you more."

Marion caught the detective's skeptical look and noted his silence. She couldn't decide: another cup of coffee would probably upset her stomach even more, but she still felt fatigued. She tried to pull herself together.

Combes, meanwhile, had opened the window and lit a Gitanes. Marion understood. She was frustrating him. This man, who cared for her in an almost fatherly way, was losing patience. How far could she go with her evasiveness and secrecy? Combes was a shrewd detective. It was possible that he was aware of much more than he was letting on.

Marion looked over at Chris, who hadn't yet gotten out of bed. His back was to them, and he had pulled the covers over his head. "Okay, I can see that I'm on my own here," she said to herself.

Combes started in again. "So, to sum things up: in the last ten days we've had two murders, one attempted drowning, sculptures that just vanish and reappear, an heiress who's so evasive she might very well inherit nothing, and a researcher who follows her around like a puppy dog. And then, perhaps most important, a detective who is being made to believe that a wealth estimated at over thirty million euros hasn't incited the slightest interest, the smallest bit of excitement."

Marion was silent. Combes was giving her one last chance to come around. But she wasn't going to give in.

"Since you're unwilling to reveal anything, I'm going to take another approach," he finally announced. "The sculptures are fakes, Marion. And Duverger knew that."

Shocked, she looked at Combes and then at Chris, who was sitting up now and shaking his head, silently telling her that he hadn't divulged a thing. How did Combes know? There wasn't any way…

"But that's not the worst part. Magni's value system wasn't the same as ours," Combes said, apparently weighing his words. "Would a madman with his resources and proclivities be satisfied with just creating fakes, aware of the small art world's willingness to do anything to protect itself?"

Marion felt her heartbeat speeding up.

"Chartier," Combes continued. "The way his body was mutilated—"

"The way his body was mutilated? What are you saying?"

"The lacerations..." Combes paused. "I wanted to talk to you about it, but you ran off. The killer reproduced the sculpture's designs on Chartier's body. And he cut off the thumb of his right hand."

Horrified, Marion hugged her knees to her chest. Her mind flashed back to Ozenberg and their lovemaking. The designs he outlined on her body.

"He engraved them on the right side of Chartier's torso. He took out his eyes and made holes in his cheeks in the same places where the emeralds were."

Marion recalled how Romarel, Magni's former lover, described the way Magni had disfigured his own face. Marion was shaking.

"Similar markings were found on bodies in Peru," the relentless detective continued. "No one there ever established a connection. We wanted to make one. They were all artisans whose deaths had never been figured out. Curiously, they lived quite close to one another in the same region of Piura. Magni had entrusted each one with creating a fake sculpture."

Combes stopped, as if to let Marion take the information in.

"But Magni wasn't alone. He had an associate. A man named Ozenberg."

Tears were streaming down Marion's face now.

"Yes, I believe you met him the other day. He had shady networks in South America, and he helped Magni carry out his plan. After making sure the men who made the sculptures were dead, your father gave Ozenberg the assignment of ensuring that they reached you and eliminating those who might get in the way. My partner from homicide arrested him this morning and will soon charge him with Chartier's murder. Nobody thought for a moment that he and Magni were in cahoots. Actually, their partnership went back further than that. Ozenberg was working for Magni for a long time—tracking down widows who had the misfortune of inheriting whatever Magni was interested in, making sure competitive collectors never got in his way and keeping tomb robbers under his thumb, all while maintaining a fairly clean front with his Paris gallery. He even bought one of the fakes at the auction to keep up appearances."

Marion buried her face in her hands.

"Marion, you need to listen. You could be seriously implicated. You have the sculptures, and they are part of a criminal investigation. You must turn them over to me."

Marion was silent.

"Say something, Marion. Everything is out in the open." The detective's tone was gentle. "I have no idea if your collection is worth anything now. Its only prestige came from having belonged to Magni. Once every sordid detail about your father and what he stooped to gets out, you'll have the job of convincing the industry that the collection still has merit. Just ask yourself if this was all worth it."

Marion stood up and wiped her face.

"You'll get the sculptures," she said. Then she threw her shoulders back and looked the detective in the eye. "Yes, it was worth it. You want to know why? Because I'll never experience another ordinary day in my life."

EPILOGUE

It wasn't six o'clock yet, and it was already hot. Someone was pounding on the door. Juan didn't feel like getting up. His ears were ringing. His eyes were scratchy, and his throat was dry.

"Juan, it's me, Miguel. Open up!"

Juan didn't respond. Maybe Miguel would go away.

"Fuck, Juan, what the hell are you doing? I know you're in there!"

Juan spat swear words into his mattress and then yelled at the door. "Get lost!"

The man on the other side banged even harder.

Juan sat up and ran a hand through his hair. His mind still foggy, he stared at his dirty feet. How long had it been since he showered?

"Juan! Juan!" Miguel persisted. "The *huaqueros*. We need you."

"All right, all right, I'm coming."

"What the fuck are you doing?" Miguel asked when Juan opened the door. He was out of breath from all the pounding. Miguel was a big man whose pants couldn't accommodate his huge belly. They rode his hips, which meant that the top of his ass crack was usually exposed, despite the loose-fitting shirts the police officer favored. "Shit, it reeks in here! What a fucking mess!"

Mango peels and empty bottles littered the floor. Dishes were strewn on the counter, and the ceramic-tile floor hadn't been swept for days.

"Yeah, I've been feeling crummy. Some kind throat thing," Juan said.

"I can see why. The ashtrays are full! So what have you been smoking?"

"I think I've got some Chicha Morado in the fridge. I haven't had anything to eat or drink in days. Let me check." He pulled out two bottles and handed one to his friend.

Miguel took a slug. "Now go get in the shower. It'll make you feel better." He watched in amusement as Juan ducked into the bathroom. "And you shouldn't hit the liquor so hard. You need to keep a closer watch on that." He absently shooed a fly away with the back of his hand.

"Tell me," Juan yelled as he sprayed himself with cold water. "What could be so urgent at this hour?"

"A seizure. I'll explain later. Once we get there. You have to see it first.

~ ~ ~

Behind the wheel of his old pickup, Miguel was flying up a badly rutted dirt road with his friend. All around, the mountain landscape looked desolate, with only a few scrubby patches of vegetation interrupting the barren soil. Suddenly, while rounding a curve, Miguel encountered a stretch of low-hanging clouds.

"Shit, that's just what we need! Juan, check to see how much room we have on our right!"

Juan, who had nodded off in the passenger seat, struggled to sit up. He looked out the window. "I can't see anything, and we're getting too high up. Let's find a place to turn around and make the trip tomorrow."

"Not gonna happen," Miguel replied dryly. "We're going up there. At five miles an hour, maybe, but we're going."

"Are you crazy? We're hugging the side of the mountain already. God help us if another pickup's coming from the other direction. We'll be screwed. Not even a stand of pine trees to break our fall." Juan crossed himself and cursed into his beard, convinced that the police were overdoing it, and the seizure wasn't worth the trouble—at least not in these conditions.

Ever since he had been appointed director of the Lambaye museum and put in charge of the province's excavations, Juan hadn't been able to study the contents of a single grave. Tomb raiders were always one step ahead of him. Today wouldn't be any different. But Miguel kept going.

Two hours and twelve miles later, Miguel stopped the engine and motioned to Juan to get out of the pickup and follow him to a stucco hut on the outskirts of a village.

Inside, the hut was dimly lit by an oil lamp. Juan could make out a wood-plank bed topped with a foam mattress and a table at the back of the room. Sculptures were resting on the table.

"I can't see worth a damn," Juan said. "Give me a flashlight. One that works."

Miguel handed over his flashlight, and Juan inspected the objects one by one. It was a real smorgasbord: red and brown funeral vases, leather masks, cups and bowls, and anthropomorphic sculptures. But there was nothing worth interrupting his sleep therapy. It was a waste of his time.

Just as he was about to turn off the flashlight and leave, he directed the beam toward a sack of potatoes. Peeping out from behind it was the head of a sculpted figure. In the figure's nose was a gold ring with an emerald. Juan gulped as he picked up the figure and carefully examined it. He couldn't believe his eyes. The craftsmanship was impeccable.

"Miguel, your *huaqueros* struck gold. Tell me what went down here."

"A fight between the Bernal brothers, most likely when they were divvying up the loot. They had been in a burial mound near the village. We nabbed one of them after the villagers notified us. The other one got away. Is it that important?"

"Look..."

The police officer let out a whistle of admiration as he turned the sculpture around in his hands. "Do you remember the Magni affair?" he asked. "This definitely looks like *The Tattooed Man*. You know, the sculpture that disappeared after his death. I didn't put much stock in the story the girl told. She thought the sculpture was cursed. That gringo Magni had just keeled over after attacking her, so I thought she was imagining things. I can see now that this fits her description."

"At least we're not going to let this one get away!" Juan said.

"What do you plan on doing with it?"

"You know exactly what I plan to do. It's not leaving the country. Not one of those sculptures has ever been seen again."

"You can't display it in your miserable museum."

"Oh yes I can. As a matter of fact, it'll be showcased in the middle of the main room."

"Are you crazy? The *huaqueros* have been digging up graves for generations. You think they won't break into your place and take it right out from under your nose?"

Juan seemed unfazed by the officer's concern. Deep in thought, he was staring at the sculpture, evaluating it, and determining how strong a punch it would bring.

"That's what they make security systems for, my friend. With this, my miserable little museum will be able to afford a security system and much more.

"People will come from all over to see it. Researchers, collectors, archeologists, scientists… Then the others will come—hundreds of visitors from all over the world. I'll have a hotel built and a library in Itauba. I'll invite guest speakers and hire a personal assistant. I'll acquire other terra-cotta sculptures and expand the museum. Nothing but the best lighting and the finest showcases. I'll devote an entire room to this single piece. And I'll finally be able to tell off anyone I want. This piece will be my most beautiful jewel, and I will be its guardian."

Thank you for reading The Collector.

We invite you to share your thoughts and reactions on Goodreads and your favorite social media and retail platforms.

We appreciate your support.

About the Author

Born in Algeria in 1963, Anne-Laure Thiéblemont grew up in Madagascar, Lyon, Paris, and Bogota. This childhood spent on the move left her with a taste for travel. That and her studies in art history were the two influences that would shape her career. She worked for a long time as an independent reporter for major French daily newspapers and magazines, specializing in art and gem trafficking. Afterward, she spent thirteen years as a magazine editor-in-chief. She lives in Marseille, France, and since 2014 has been working on her own design and applied arts magazine. Writing is her passion, her own secret garden. *The Collector* is her first mystery and was inspired from her investigative reporting on art trafficking and meetings she had with famous art collectors. When Anne-Laure is not writing, she is out searching for gems and designing jewelry she has made in Istanbul.

About the Translator

Sophie Weiner is a freelance translator and book publishing assistant from Baltimore, Maryland. After earning degrees in French from Bucknell University and New York University, Sophie went on to complete a master's in literary translation from the Sorbonne, where she focused her thesis on translating wordplay in works by Oulipo authors. She has translated and written for web-based companies dedicated to art, cinema, and fashion, as well as for nonprofit organizations. Growing up with *Babar*, *Madeline*, and *The Little Prince*, Sophie was bitten by the Francophile bug at an early age, and is fortunate enough to have lived in Paris, Lille, and the Loire Valley.

About Le French Book

Le French Book is a New York-based publisher specializing in great reads from France. It was founded in December 2011 because, as founder Anne Trager says, "I couldn't stand it anymore. There are just too many good books not reaching a broader audience. There is a very vibrant, creative culture in France, and we want to get them out to more readers."

www.lefrenchbook.com